Casting Vows

HEARTS OF GOLD
BOOK THREE

ARIELLA TALIX

Ariella Talix

Copyright © 2024 Ariella Talix, all rights reserved.
Ringmaster Publishing

Never let your sense of morals prevent you from doing what is right.
—Isaac Asimov

Introduction and Trigger Warnings

Dear Reader,

The attitudes toward women portrayed in this book reflect the prevailing opinions of the late nineteenth century. Please keep this in mind as you read. I will not whitewash history to make the story more palatable for a twenty-first century sensibility. Some characters are more enlightened than others because of their personalities.

In all cases, I did a tremendous amount of research and tried to keep the language and opinions true to the times. This was quite the education as often words or phrases that sound old to us are actually new, and vice versa. For example, "full tilt" dates from the sixteenth century, whereas "troublemaker" is a twentieth-century addition to our vocabulary.

I hope you learn to love these characters as I do.

There may be triggers in this story for some readers,

detailed in the paragraph below. If you don't want to read any spoilers, stop reading here and go on to the story.

If you are worried about triggers, these include child abuse (<u>not</u> sexual), violence, and alcoholism. If these topics bother you too much to read about, I am sorry, and I understand. I don't want anyone to be distressed.

Ariella Talix

PART

One

CHAPTER
One

Los Angeles, 1884. The year the rain would not stop.

What's going on out there? Nicolo Stark-James asked himself, sitting up and rubbing sleepily at his eyes. The rainfall made a racket, but Nico was sure he had heard a strange thud against his bedroom window.

It was around midnight, and the torrential rain had made a mess of the property outside their ranch-style home. The usually mild California weather had suddenly turned nasty, and rain had been falling constantly for two solid weeks. The deluge created a muddy quagmire that was nearly impossible to navigate where they lived, but in other parts of Los Angeles, the flood was submerging orchards and carrying houses away. At least two hundred houses had been swept away along with outbuildings and fences, causing hundreds of residents to seek shelter.

Nico went to the window and shoved the curtain out of the way. Rain cascaded down the glass, but through the distortion, he could make out the shape of his best friend, hunched over in an odd position, boots sunk deep into the mud just beneath Nico's window.

Immediately, Nico raised the pane—he never bothered to lock the window—and snapped at Matty, "Why are you waiting out there? Climb on in like you always do!"

"Can't. Need help." Matty's voice was weak and shook with emotion and apparent agony that set Nico's senses on alert. He clutched his belly and wasn't raising his face to look at Nico.

Oh no. It happened again.

Not wanting to take time for an explanation, Nico asked, "Can you give me your hand and let me pull you in?"

Matty groaned and shook his head stiffly.

"Then meet me at the front door. Can you make it that far?" Matty was swaying. "I'll get one of my fathers to help!"

"No! You promised. I don't want more trouble with..." At that, Matty puked up something that looked an awful lot like blood and collapsed in a heap, landing in the mud with a splat.

Sometimes, it's prudent to break a promise, even if it's to your best friend in the whole world. Matty was as important to Nico as his own family. He loved him—not like a brother. Of course, he loved his brothers Bay and Warren as well as his sisters Ondine and Martha, but he loved Matty with a depth of affection he had never tried to analyze. He just knew he had to take care of Matty and had to do it *now*. Leaving the window open, allowing the rain to soak the curtains and the floor, he dashed out of his room and down the hall.

Originally built for three married adults, five children—four of whom were now married and gone—frequent house-guests, and a good-sized household staff, the estate was a huge, rambling one-story design built in the Mexican-inspired Hacienda style popular in the southern part of California. Thick stucco-covered adobe walls made the house cool in the summer. The property was surrounded by a high wall covered with a splendid display of brilliantly hued bougainvillea. The gate was generally left open for their frequent guests who came for a concert or a meal.

Nico's two fathers Walter and Isaac owned half of a successful building firm with their best friends Jasper Langley and Royal Dawson, and they'd learned to adapt their architectural style to suit the area rather than trying to replicate the grand wooden houses they'd built in the north. They'd all been living in San Francisco for several years but emigrated south when they decided it was time for new challenges and adventures.

The move south had been good for them. Originally, they'd made their fortunes as the earliest, hardest-working miners in the 1849 California Gold Rush, then as successful hotel and casino owners, and ultimately as a topnotch building company they called Roja Wais. Their pioneering spirit prompted them to finally move south to seek new opportunities. In doing so, they increased their fortune even more with their current business, which they had named New West Builders. Their closest friends and best workers made the southern trek with them with the exception of Séamus Flynn and Timothy Duffy who remained in San Francisco and continued to run The Discovery Hotel and Casino with several of their Irish relatives.

Nico's bedroom was quite a distance from his three parents' room, so by the time he got there after running full tilt—and gripped with terror—he was gasping for breath. Not thinking, but desperately needing help, he shoved the heavy arched door open, rushed in, and gaped at the strangest sight.

As the thick door swung inward with a creak and Nico charged in, the three occupants' startled faces turned to their son in shock. They had not been sleeping. Nico's mother Suzette was as naked as her two husbands, and they were doing things Nico had not ever imagined. Still, no matter what his parents were getting up to—and frankly it looked pretty interesting—he had to help Matty *now*.

"I need your help!" he nearly sobbed. "Matty's outside and he's sick or hurt something *bad*. Please hurry!"

Isaac pulled away from Walter, and Nico tried not to look as his pa's rigid cock lost its stiffness. Isaac reached for a pair of trousers and yanked them on. "Show me where he is, son," he ordered. Isaac didn't bother with a shirt or boots. Nico's terror was apparently enough to convince him that this matter was dire.

As Isaac hastily did up his trousers, Walter and Suzette disengaged a bit more slowly. Walter tossed a dressing gown to her and found something to put on, saying, "This is precisely why we need to have a telephone installed. I'll go get Doc Louis. Get that poor boy inside and out of the elements."

Nico dashed outside and swam through the rain, not even feeling it as he directed his father to just outside his bedroom window. They discovered Matty looking very, *very* bad. He hadn't moved a muscle since he collapsed.

"Run back in and tell your mother to get some hot water and blankets for him, Nicolo. I'll try to carry him in without hurting him." Isaac was a large bear of a man, strong and fearless, but as gentle as a lamb when he needed to be.

Nico watched nervously as Isaac bent to scoop Matty up into his arms, cradling him to his broad chest, and then Nico tore off again, running as quickly as possible through the slimy mud to fetch his mother. He nearly collided with Walter at the front door.

"Did Isaac find him, son?"

"Yessir, Papa. Pa's carrying him in now. Matty isn't moving though," he added with a hitch in his voice. He was scared to death that Matty wasn't breathing.

"I'll be back as soon as I can rouse Doc Louis. I just have to navigate through this mess somehow. This must be one of those hundred-year storms I've read about. Oh, I hope Doc Louis hasn't been called away somewhere else…" Walter was still talking nonstop as he streaked out the door toward the street. He carried an umbrella—not that it did much good in sideways rain. Before he made it a hundred feet, the umbrella blew inside out and flew away to join the downed trees and general detritus caused by the flood.

Nico missed most of Walter's ramblings as he ran in to alert his mother.

Suzette was already in the kitchen with the cook, and they were heating water and setting out clean rags and towels. Isaac met them with the seemingly lifeless body in his arms, and he carefully lay Matty down on the large worktable as Nico turned on the combination gas and electric lights and lit some candles around the room for extra illumination. The women began to remove Matty's filthy boots and sodden clothing. He was streaked with mud—and blood—and dripping rainwater everywhere.

Isaac lay his head on Matty's chest and pronounced, "He has a good, strong heartbeat, Nicolo. Don't worry. Doc Louis will help him. He's the best there is on fixing people up. He's getting on in years, but he's done a great job on me a time or two."

Nico was aware of the story that caused the scar over his pa's eyebrow. It had faded a lot over the years, but he agreed with his mother that the scar made Isaac look rugged and a little dangerous. Isaac stood back and went about cleaning as much of the mud as he could off of himself.

Matty's face was terribly beaten up, but when they opened Matty's shirt, Suzette gave a gasp and said some choice words in French. Everyone knew immediately she was furious—especially Nico who'd been raised speaking French as well as English. "Look at this poor child!" She pointed to a blossoming bruise at the base of the young man's ribcage that looked suspiciously like Matty had been kicked—probably multiple times. Suzette wiped an angry tear from her face.

"He was vomiting blood, Maman," Nico said in an unsteady voice. "Do you really think he'll get well?"

"As long as he stays away from that dreadful father of his, yes."

"You know about Matty's father?"

Isaac spoke up, "We all do, son. We've just been unable to do much about it. We've tried talking to him, but… no luck. However, this time… the man has gone too far, and I plan to speak to the police. I'm guessing they'll be too busy right now to do much, considering the looting and property destruction going on during this storm. But that awful man could have killed his own son. He's a nasty old drunk and as mean as a snake. I'm so sorry Matty's mother isn't around to care for him anymore."

Feeling powerless to help his friend, Nico fought back angry tears and decided to do the one thing he felt would please Matty.

He prayed the way he'd been taught by the Vincentian fathers at the school where he and Matty were day students. He prayed for Matty to wake up and not be in terrible pain. He prayed for Papa to get Doc Louis to the house soon. He prayed Matty would make a full recovery and be able to enjoy life, and he prayed for Matty's father to burn in hell for his sins. Nico wasn't sure one ought to pray for that, but he couldn't help himself, and if the God whom Matty loved so much had any sense, he would understand.

Matty would know the value of such a prayer. He was always the faithful one. Where Nico—a fairly non-religious person—generally breezed through life looking for ways to be amused, Matty looked at the world as God's beautiful creation and considered how best to live his life as a good, faithful Catholic. Matty's devotion had deepened after his mother died, and Nico figured his friend needed his faith to sustain him through his grief of losing her. Nico had been baptized and once in a while attended mass and took holy communion, but he just went through the motions of being faithful—sometimes to please his mother, but even more often to please Matty.

Unfortunately, Matty's father, who lived off his considerable inheritance, sought his solace for losing his wife in the bottom of a whiskey bottle. His idle lifestyle and drinking turned him cantankerous, and if Matty—his only child—happened to be handy, he became the target of the man's wrath. Usually, it was just words—horrible, cutting words—that often included blaming Matty for making his mother sick and causing her to die. It was irrational, but that didn't make it hurt any less. Worse still, when the man's mental anguish got to be too bad, his belligerence turned physical.

There was no doubt in Nico's mind that Matty needed to get away from his father before he joined his mother prematurely. But any time Nico brought it up, tender-hearted Matty shook his head. His father needed him, Matty explained.

Matty studied hard at school each day, but when classes were finished, he ran home to see if his father was getting into trouble. The staff he'd had was dwindling—moving off to find better employment with a more reasonable boss—and there was not much Matty could do to get them to stay. So he took to watching his father to make sure the man didn't either drink himself to death or starve. He routinely watered down the liquor bottles and tried to force his father to eat solid food, but he had rather poor luck with both ventures.

Often after his father passed out for the night, Matty would walk over to the house where Nico lived. He would climb in through Nico's bedroom window and the two of them would talk for hours. More than once, he'd fallen asleep in Nico's bed with him. Nico was his solace. Matty adored his friend and often wished he could live there with Nico's unconventional, loving family. But even if they'd invited him, Matty knew he couldn't abandon his sick father. Still, now that school was on a break because of the flood, he'd been spending more time with Nico, and he loved that too.

♡♡♡

By the time Walter and Doc Louis made it back to the house, Matty was cleaned up and starting to come around. His nose was still bleeding, though, and he once again puked up a bloody mess and writhed in agony. Doc Louis took one look at his patient and started swearing crudely in French. Methodically, he began the process of evaluating Matty's injuries.

"It appears he has a broken nose, and the blood he is vomiting up probably has to do with all he has swallowed from that. I do not believe the abdominal injuries are severe enough to have caused internal bleeding, but he does have what looks like a couple of busted ribs. That is going to be terribly painful for a while, and he will need to remain quiet for a couple of weeks before he can walk around freely. Can you keep him here? We cannot allow him to be reinjured." The implication was strong that Doc Louis was also aware Matty was the victim of his father's wrath.

"Yes, of course," Suzette replied. "We can put him in Bay's old room now that he's moved out."

"No!" Nico interrupted. "Please put him in my room. I'll be there to take care of him and watch over him. He needs me."

"That's fine, Nicolo," Isaac said. "He'll be happy to be with you."

Looking at Doc Louis, Nico implored, "Please, can you give him something for the pain, sir?"

"Oui, I shall. However, I do not wish to upset his stomach. Each time he retches, it will cause him tremendous pain. So we will need to treat him somewhat conservatively. I will give him something now so he will sleep, and I can set his broken nose. He will probably sleep for a few hours, but you will need to administer this when he wakes and every few hours throughout the next days." He handed Nico a packet, saying, "This will diminish his pain. We will only use a small amount for a short time, and then we will switch to this." They had a conversation about how to handle the drugs and how to best help Matty move around eventually.

Doc Louis noticed Nico's close attention to everything he said and listened to Nico's detailed questions which finally prompted him to ask, "Nicolo, would you consider studying with me? I've been thinking for a while that you may have the makings of a future doctor. You could try medicine out as an apprentice and then enter medical school if the subject suits you."

Nico's chin dropped. He was flattered Doc Louis held him in such high regard. In truth, he'd always been curious about how the body worked, and the few times he'd seen Doc Louis' office at the clinic, he was fascinated. "Uh… yes sir," he answered somewhat breathlessly. He looked at each of his three parents and saw expressions of pride on their faces.

Up to now, Nico had always felt like an oddity in his family. His siblings were considerably older than him, and each of them played a variety of instruments beautifully and with great passion. His pa Isaac and his mother were extraordinary violinists, and their close friend Adeline Dawson-Langley was a fabulous pianist who collaborated and taught with them. For some reason, however, Nicolo, inaptly named for Nicolo Paganini, demonstrated no musical talent whatsoever. It was the one thing about himself that made him believe his actual father was Walter, the only other non-musician in the family. He didn't particularly care whether he was the son of Isaac or Walter; they both loved him fiercely, he knew, just as he loved them. But it was lonely for him when his siblings congregated and put on fabulous concerts with his mother and Isaac. They all enjoyed it so much, while he just couldn't find any music within himself. The irony of his namesake was not lost on him, so he always introduced himself as Nico rather than Nicolo, fearing the more formal version of his name might prompt questions he was too embarrassed to address.

But now! Could it be that he had his own personal calling? He looked at Doc Louis and said, "Thank you, sir!"

"How are your marks at school?" the old man asked.

"Good sir, but I can do better, I promise!"

"You *must* keep that promise, Nicolo. Learn as much as you can from the good priests. But we shall also see how you care for Matty here, and when he is better, you will come to the clinic and work with me after school—as long as your parents agree, of course. It will not be terribly interesting at first and a considerable amount of hard work. I also have many books you will want to read, and I can prepare you for medical school this way."

"Well," exclaimed Walter as he beamed at his son. "Isn't that grand?" Walter was in favor of anything that involved learning and books. "Thank you, Doc Louis."

Nico couldn't help but think tonight had been one of the worst in his life because he'd been tremendously worried about Matty and furious on his behalf for what Mr. Remington had done. Now, as the dawn was breaking, the night turned into something far more promising. He couldn't wait to tell Matty when his friend was conscious again.

CHAPTER
Two

Once Doc Louis finished with Matty, Isaac again carefully picked him up and carried him into Nico's room. Possibly because of his own large frame, Isaac had built larger than normal beds for all the rooms in the house. After settling Matty into Nico's good-sized bed that could comfortably accommodate two sixteen-year-old boys, Isaac saw the concern on Nico's face and asked, "Do you need to get some rest, son, or are you hungry? Matty's going to sleep a while, so you don't need to stay here with him all the time."

"I think I could eat, but I'm awfully tired too."

Isaac nodded. "Let's grab some breakfast and then we can all get some rest. It's been a harrowing night for everyone. I hope Walter has changed out of his soaking clothes by now. And I think your mother is planning to insist Doc Louis take a rest in one of the bedrooms as well." Isaac suddenly looked surprised. "Nicolo! Do you hear that?"

Pulling on his trousers, Nico answered, "Hear what? I don't hear a thing."

"Precisely! It's stopped raining! Oh, I hope this lasts. We've had enough rain for three or four years, and the devastation is horrible." He affectionately slung his arm around Nico's shoulders, and they made their way back to the dining room where Suzette cheerfully chatted with Doc Louis.

To look at her, you'd never guess that she too had been up all night. With a lovely smile, she regarded her husband and son as they sat down. "Look! We have blue sky this morning," she beamed.

"And I shall take advantage of this break in the weather and head for home," Doc Louis announced.

"Can you stay long enough to have coffee and a bit to eat?" Suzette asked.

"Thank you, but my dearest Marguerite is waiting for me, and I shall take my leave. Please let me know if Matty needs me for any reason. I will be back tomorrow to check on him."

Unfortunately, the sunny respite did not last more than a few minutes, and Doc Louis got soaked through before he reached home. Once the rain began again, it did not stop for another week. Homes were destroyed, and property was ruined; it was a wonder more people didn't perish. Storms would continue that year from late January until May with the highest cumulative rainfall ever recorded. The Stark-James family and all of their friends and relatives could not have been more relieved that they'd chosen property far away from the Los Angeles River or any low-lying areas.

In the meantime, after finishing breakfast, Nico could barely keep his eyes open. Suzette ordered him to bed, saying, "Let us know if Matty wakes up and needs some food or help to the toilet, or anything. Do not try to do everything yourself, Nicolo. You need to stay healthy too."

"Yes, Maman." Nico looked at her and then at his two fathers and added, "Thank you for helping Matty. I love you all so much. I wish Matty had parents like I have."

"Well, at least he has a friend who loves him," Walter said with a kind smile. "Without your interference, there is no telling what may have happened to the poor young man. I'm glad he came to you." Turning to Isaac, he added, "We just have to figure out what to do about that hideous man now, so Matty remains safe." Looking at his son, he asked, "Does Matty's father know how much time he spends over here with you, Nicolo?"

"Oh, I doubt it. Matty usually waits until Mr. Remington has passed out before he leaves him. But there have been a few times he's asked in the morning where Matty was. He said he usually tells his father something like, 'I went for a walk' because he doesn't want to involve us in his trouble with his father. But..." Nico lowered his head like the subject pained him. "He doesn't like lying to his father. He told me he's had to go to confession about it several times."

There was an audible collective sigh from all three parents, and Isaac spoke up. "That young man has too many problems to worry about, and his eternal soul should not be one of them. I'll have a talk with him when he's feeling up to it. Now go get some sleep, son. You look dead on your feet. And, Nicolo, we're proud of you and what a good friend you are to him."

Nico embraced his fathers and kissed his mother, then shuffled down the long, tiled hallway to his room rubbing his eyes as he went. His head swam, he was so tired. *Thank goodness I don't have to attend school today,* he thought to himself. *I'd be worthless.*

Nico tried to be silent as he entered his bedroom, drew the curtains closed, and climbed into bed beside Matty. In the dim light, he scowled at how much worse the bruising on Matty's normally handsome face looked. He had two black eyes and swelling where Doc Louis had done repair work to Matty's nose. *It's a wonder Matty still has all of his teeth. I could strangle that so-called father of his. I wonder if Matty ever fights back against that monster.* Looking at Matty's hand, he was frustrated not to see any bruising or cuts on his knuckles, but Nico struggled to subdue the tears that threatened to fall as he thought of how beautiful his friend was inside and out. Matty had thick, wavy black hair and eyes the color of the summer sky. His features were so perfect, Nico often thought Matty should have been a prince or a knight, or some heroic champion in a story—not a victim for a mean drunk to pound on.

Growing up as he had in a house with a mother and two fathers who routinely showed affection to one another, and being close friends with another such family, Nico didn't think twice about demonstrating his fondness for Matty. They had been best friends for years, and Nico knew in his heart that he loved Matty. No one was gentler, kinder, more steadfast, or loyal. Desperately needing to touch him without disturbing his friend, Nico reached out and gently stroked a lock of hair off his forehead. Nico knew sleep was the best thing. As long as Matty slept, he would not feel the pain in his ribs or his poor face, so Nico scooted back a little, kissed Matty's shoulder, and lay his head over the kissed spot. He whispered, "I love you, Matty. Please get better soon." Nico fell into exhausted sleep in less than two minutes.

♡♡♡

ABOUT FOUR HOURS LATER, NICO AWOKE WITH A START. Matty was moaning and trying to get up.

"Hold on. What's the matter?" he asked.

"Toilet." Matty's voice sounded muffled and miserable. Nico figured it was partially due to the cotton packed into his nose.

"I'll help you. Just a second." Nico sprang out of bed and gently put his arm behind Matty so he could help him sit up.

After lots of grimacing and cries of pain, they finally got Matty to the bathroom Nico shared with his brothers where he took care of business. "I'm so sorry you're hurting, Matty. Doc Louis gave me some medicine to help you and said for me to give it to you when you woke up."

Walking sapped Matty's energy, and he didn't want to talk quite yet, so he just nodded his head a little. Once they had him situated back in the bed, Nico carefully measured out what Doc Louis said to give him and administered it to Matty. "This will help, but tonight I'll give you a little opium so you can sleep," he explained. "It's for the first couple of days only, and then we'll just use the milder medicine. Hopefully you'll sleep a lot, and that will help you get better. Are you hungry?"

Matty looked at Nico with sad, bloodshot eyes. "Not so much," he whispered. "Stay with me?"

"I will, but I need to go get you something to drink at least. Doc Louis said it would make you feel better to have something in your stomach. Maybe the cook has some broth. I promise, I'll be right back as soon as I can."

As Nico stood to go, Matty grabbed his hand. "What if my father shows up here? I don't want any trouble for your family. He could try to hurt someone here."

"Do you think he knows where you've gone?"

"I sure didn't tell him, but maybe someone saw me."

"They'd have to be a pretty awful person to let him know in that case, and it was in the middle of the night. How did you even get here when you were in such terrible shape?"

Matty sighed and then winced from the deep breath. "It took me a long time to make it. I couldn't breathe very well, and at one point I was afraid I'd drown when I tripped and landed in a big puddle. That hurt *so* badly, but I just hauled myself up and kept putting one foot in front of the other. I *had* to get away from that house." A tear rolled down his cheek. "I was so scared, Nico. He's never been that violent before, and I was afraid this time he might kill me. I don't even know what set him off originally, but he got angrier than usual because I fought back this time." He hung his head. "He was taunting me, but I tried to ignore him, so he punched me in the nose." Matty paused for a moment. "I felt it break, and I thought my head would explode from the pain, so I struck him back without even thinking. I only hit him with an open hand, but he went into a fury. He knocked me down and started kicking me. I was in so much pain, I couldn't even get up to defend myself at that point, but he was drunk and finally wore himself out." Tears poured freely down Matty's face at this point. "When he turned away from me to grab his whiskey bottle, I shoved him. He fell down, and I think he hit his head, so I left as quickly as I could." Matty suddenly looked horrified. "I hope I didn't kill him!"

Nico felt like crying seeing Matty in such anguish. On some level, Matty must still care for his father, but he was also scared to death for his own safety. It was so typical of Matty to worry about a man who'd brutally attacked him. "Don't worry, Matty. If he was that drunk, he probably just passed out and hopefully won't remember what happened. My fathers will keep you safe here. They promised me." He squeezed Matty's hand. "I'll be right back with some soup for you. Please don't worry." He knew that request was going to have little if any effect on Matty's thinking, but he had to try.

A few minutes later, Nico was back with a tray from the kitchen, followed by his mother.

"How do you feel, Matty?" she asked. "I am glad to see you are awake now."

"Oh, I've definitely had better days than this, ma'am, but I'll be alright. Thank you for your kindness."

"Matty, you are like another son to me. You are welcome to stay here to recuperate. I must tell you that my husbands left a little while ago to speak to the police on your behalf, but with this weather disaster we are having, the officers are over-burdened right now. Despite the fact that we now have laws that prevent cruelty to children in this country, and they are no longer seen as property of their parents, I do not know how much assistance the police will be able to provide. We will discuss the possibilities for keeping you safe when Walter and Isaac return. Now, please have some of this delicious hot soup, and then get some rest." She stroked a hand lovingly through his hair as she had done so many times since he was a young boy, and it never failed to make Matty miss his own mother terribly.

"Yes, ma'am." Then a terrible thought occurred to Matty. "Is the house unprotected with Mr. Isaac and Mr. Walter gone?

I'm so afraid my father will guess where I am and cause you trouble."

"Do not worry. Our dear Jeb Hawkins is guarding the front gate, and the men locked it when they left. Your father would have a very difficult time getting in today." Normally, the gate was left standing open to welcome their family and friends, but hearing that Isaac and Walter had taken this precaution made Matty relax. He also knew what a trusted friend Jeb Hawkins was, and considering that the man dwarfed Isaac with his impressive size, Matty imagined Jeb could handle his father. He'd even heard the story about how Jeb had saved Suzette's life before he'd moved south with everyone.

Suzette recognized the relief on Matty's face. "So have your soup and then rest, my sweet boy. Our entire family wants to see you feel better quickly. Isaac and Walter will let you know what the police say, if anything."

"Do you think they will arrest my father?"

"I would not know. Do not think about it now. Have some food and get some rest. The cook served enough for both of you two to enjoy, and she baked a very fine cake if you want something sweet. I will leave you now and go check with our guard to see if he has seen anything suspicious. He might also want hot coffee after standing out in the rain."

"Oh, I feel like I'm causing all sorts of trouble for your family, ma'am. Maybe I ought to just go home and face my father like a man."

"Absolutely not!" Suzette gasped.

"No!" Nico cried at the same time. "He might actually kill you!"

"Matty," Suzette said softly, "do not think of such a thing. We are happy to protect and keep you. The men will figure out something. Do not worry about us."

Just then, they all heard the unmistakable sound of a shotgun blast.

CHAPTER
Three

Nico raced to the front door while Suzette loudly cautioned him, "Stay in the house, Nicolo, and let Jeb handle it! You do not want to be caught in the middle of a gun fight."

Understanding the gravity of his mother's warning, Nico merely opened the door a crack and peeked out to see Jeb looking thunderous out in the pouring rain. He was shouting at someone, "I told you to get the hell away from this house now!"

Matty's father stood outside the gate. Nico held his breath as Mr. Remington shouted repulsive curses at Jeb and then turned to stomp away hollering that it was against the law to kidnap his "precious son," and he would see to it that they would all pay for this.

With the danger gone, Nico had to laugh at the man's parting words. "Precious," eh? That was a good one. Never

ever had that man shown any care toward Matty. The only thing Mr. Remington liked about Matty was that he made a good target for his punches, and Matty willingly ran errands for the awful man. At least he was leaving the premises. For now.

"Are you alright, Jeb?" Nico called through the rain.

Jeb turned and saw Nico and stomped toward the door. "Stay inside, boy. That man has lost his senses, and he's drunk. There's no telling what he'll do. I didn't shoot to harm him. I just fired into the air… this time. I only meant to scare him off, but he kept coming toward me. I hope next time he doesn't plan to come back with a gun."

"Yessir, Mr. Hawkins. Would you like some hot coffee to warm up?"

"No, thank you, son. I don't want to leave the house unguarded or have my attention diverted. Now get back in and tell that poor friend of yours to concentrate on getting better and not fret about that fool of a father of his. If Remington ends up getting himself arrested or killed, the world might be better off. For now, we'll just keep him off his son."

A rattling sound turned their attention to the gate. Walter was using a key to get in. He and Isaac had grim expressions on their faces. Walter carefully relocked the gate as soon as they entered.

"We saw Mr. Remington leaving the place," Isaac said. "He wandered into some deep mud just up the street and seemed too drunk to get out of it again. Needless to say, we weren't neighborly enough to help the man after hearing a gunshot from the direction of our house. I think the man actually passed out after cursing at us. Everyone here is unharmed, right Jeb? You both look calm enough."

"Everyone is fine. If that scoundrel is actually unconscious, maybe I will take a few minutes to come in and get dry. The offer of a steaming cup of hot coffee does sound good after all."

"Is Matty awake, Nico?" Isaac asked.

"Yessir. I left him with some soup, and Maman was with him in my bedroom. He should still be awake."

"Tell him we'll change into dry clothes and come speak with him shortly then."

Matty hadn't touched much of the soup when Nico found him. He looked pale and worried and asked immediately, "Was anyone shot?"

"Nah. Don't worry. I guess your father was causing a commotion and threatening Jeb Hawkins, so Jeb fired the gun to let him know he meant business when he told your pa to get lost. My fathers saw your pa a few minutes later up the street where he'd stumbled into a mud bog and passed out." Matty nodded at Nico, looking serious. "My fathers said to tell you they needed dry clothes, but they'll be in to talk to you in a few minutes about the police."

"Nico, please eat some lunch while you are waiting for your fathers. And Matty, please eat some more. Both of you need to stop fretting so much. This will all work itself out. You'll see," Suzette told them in a soothing voice.

"Yes, Maman." Nico understood that she was trying to be optimistic and not worry Matty overmuch, but he also knew his mother was only smoothing over a nearly impossible situation. He tucked into his soup to make her happy and hopefully to inspire Matty to do the same.

His plan worked a little. Matty had a bit more soup and ate a few bites of cake before Isaac and Walter showed up. They looked serious, causing Nico's optimism to bottom out.

Walter cleared his throat and said, "It's good to see you awake, Matty. I must say, you had us all in quite a panic for you last night."

Matty grimaced and answered, "Thank you, Mr. Walter."

"Yes, well." Walter sighed. "You know that Isaac and I went out earlier today to speak to the police. We stopped by and asked Doc Louis to accompany us in case we needed a witness to the… uh… goings on with you. He happily obliged us." Walter looked around and then scooted a chair up to the bed so he could speak directly to Matty—eye to eye. "Your father had already been to the police office to report that you tried to beat him up last night and fled after leaving him for dead. He wanted them to arrest you and suggested they look for you here."

Matty gasped and then cried out and grabbed his ribs, screwing up his face in agony.

Nico cried, "No! That isn't what happened at all! Mr. Remington is the one who should be arrested!"

Isaac reached for Nico and put his arm around him. "We understand, son. Relax and listen to what Walter has to say."

Walter continued, "Doc Louis looked at that policeman dead in the eye and asked him, 'Did you see any marks or bruising on Mr. Remington that would indicate he'd been beaten nearly to death… or at *all*? Because I treated his son, and that boy was nearly killed by Remington's fists and boots.' He told the officer you had a smashed nose he had to reset and at least two broken ribs where that savage kicked you repeatedly. He told them you were nearly dead when Isaac found you. The policeman said Remington had a small scratch on his cheek, but that was all he could see. He also conceded that the man reeked of alcohol but seemed to be walking around fairly well—certainly not as if favoring any part of his body. We pointed out that if he'd scraped his face, it was likely due to falling down while drunk."

"He did fall down," Matty said in a small voice. "That was how I was able finally to get away from him."

"Yes, son. And we're exceptionally proud of you for getting out of that house and coming here so we can help you. However, there is a wrinkle in the situation. The policeman told us we have no right to keep you here away from your father."

Suzette gasped, and Nico looked furious. Matty's eyes went wide with terror.

"Don't worry. Doc Louis came to your rescue, again. Bless the man. He explained that too much moving around might cause your broken ribs to puncture a lung, and that could kill you. He told the police you have to stay put for at least a month. He also suggested that you might want to press charges against your father for battery, and they could arrest *him*. Having said that, the policeman explained though that your father would probably not have to stay in jail until a trial happened, so having him arrested would not do much to save you from the man. He also pointed out that minors have very little chance of winning against abusive parents, especially those with deep pockets."

Walter paused as everyone in the room looked deflated, especially Matty. Then Isaac spoke up and said, "I think I have an idea."

CHAPTER
Four

"You can't go back to that man, Matty," Isaac explained. "He's out of his mind. But we can keep you here and keep you safe. Even if your father demands to come and visit you, we will never let him be alone with you for one minute, I promise you. He will be thoroughly checked for weapons before he is allowed into this house, and you will be guarded all the time by our men. I think he'll simmer down after a few days and a few bottles of whiskey anyway. When you are feeling strong enough to travel, we'll see to it that you are sent somewhere safe."

Nico's attention snapped to his father. "Pa! You would send Matty *away*?"

"It is not safe for him to be around that man, Nico. And eventually we're all going to have to be able to get back to our normal lives. We'll keep him safe, and then we'll figure something out. I know it sounds bad to you now, but I think it's the best thing for everyone. I'm not trying to punish either of you for anything, and I know how close you are with each other, but this is for Matty's safety." Isaac could see the devastation in their eyes. "Maybe we can find a good school for him to attend and not let his father know. I don't know. I just know that this can't go on. Mr. Remington might do some serious, irreversible harm to Matty. Or himself."

"Well, hurting himself wouldn't be so bad," Nico muttered under his breath. Then he looked into Matty's eyes and saw the fear and sadness in them. He clutched his friend's hand.

Matty spoke up. "He hasn't always been a bad father. When my mother was alive, I remember him being nice to me." Then his face crumpled, and he fought the tears that threatened to fall.

Suzette spoke up, "Nico, has Matty had anything for his pain recently?"

"Yes, ma'am. Less than an hour ago."

"Good. Then maybe we ought to let him get some rest. He has had a terrible experience, and it is too soon to be making hasty decisions while he is still in so much discomfort." She looked at her husbands with narrowed eyes. "You both probably need to eat as well. We should leave Nicolo and Matty to relax now." The look in her eyes clearly told her husbands to knock it off. There would be no discussion of sending Matty away for now. As they stepped out into the hallway, Nico clearly heard his mother scolding, "I cannot believe you two.

Can you not be a little more sensitive about those boys' feelings?"

"We offered to keep him here," muttered Isaac.

"Yes, for a limited amount of time. And then you practically ordered Matty away as soon as possible." Her voice trailed off as they made their way down the hall.

Nico saw that Matty's eyes were at half-mast. Feeling exhausted as well, he picked up the food tray and speedily took it back to the kitchen. He jogged back to Matty and climbed into bed with him, curling himself around his best friend carefully. The thought of not seeing Matty—for whatever reason—made his chest hurt. He almost looked down to see if he'd been stabbed.

Nico slept for about an hour, but when he awoke feeling refreshed, Matty slept on. So Nico took the opportunity to get himself cleaned up and properly dressed and then selected a book to read out of Walter's library. This one was about modern medical advancements. He figured he might want to get a head start on Doc Louis' plan. He also wanted to gauge his own level of interest in the topic. Much to his delight, he found the book intriguing. Sitting in his favorite chair next to the bed where Matty slept, he became so engrossed in the reading that he lost himself and temporarily forgot to be worried.

This set up a pattern they followed for the next several days. Matty slept a lot, especially at night after he was given his dose of opium. He didn't speak much and still seemed to be in considerable pain when he was awake.

On the third day, Doc Louis removed the packing from his nose, and Matty was more comfortable talking after that. Gradually, Doc Louis reduced the dose of opium, and Matty was able to sleep at night without it. He could sit up better and needed less help to get to the toilet.

Noting his progress, Doc Louis encouraged him to get up and walk around the house as much as he could tolerate. At first Nico helped him, but Matty was soon able to navigate on his own. It was slow walking, but he was happy to be up and about instead of lying in bed all the time. He took his meals with everyone in the dining room, and that made him feel like part of the human race again, even if it pained him and wore him out. The conversations at dinner were so lively, and you never knew how many guests there would be, so it was always interesting.

The subject of leaving their home was not brought up again in front of Nico and Matty.

Nico was having the time of his life. He had his best friend with him constantly. While Matty slept a lot, Nico had a stack of incredibly interesting books to read. These were courtesy of his papa's penchant for collecting books on the newest and greatest topics and from Doc Louis who dragged a bunch of books over for Nico to study. School was still not in session because the building had flooded and needed serious repairs before the students could safely return to class.

The rain continued. While some people complained about feeling trapped indoors all the time, Nico was happy.

In order to liven the spirits of those around them during this awful flood, the Stark-James family filled their evenings with guests. They played music and entertained as often as they could. All sorts of rain-soaked friends would show up for a meal and a good time, and all were welcome. The family was open about the situation Matty was in because they never wanted to appear that they were keeping him against the will of his father. They let people know Mr. Remington had been apprised of the whereabouts of his son and that he could not safely be moved to another location until his doctor gave him clearance. And of course, Doc Louis was extra conservative with his recommendations.

Isaac and Walter had paid Remington a visit and explained things in clear and stern terms: Matty would not be moved, and Remington was welcome to visit as long as he submitted to a body search for weapons before he entered their home. He also would not be left alone with Matty. So far, even though he grumbled a lot, Remington had not made the trip over to their house. He also did not express any thanks that they were taking care of his son. He was certainly not a shining example of a man.

One of the frequent guests whom Matty enjoyed was the local parish priest, Father Andrew. He often came to dine, and Matty would sit next to him. They had many philosophical discussions about world religions and the Bible, and Father

Andrew never ceased to be impressed with Matty's knowledge and ability to reason things out sensibly. One memorable night, Matty and the Father were having a discussion about the Ten Commandments. The conversation came to a brief halt when Matty choked when he thought he was supposed to love his father and his mother. He had no problem with his mother, but his father was a different story.

"We are directed by God to *honor* our fathers, Matty. You aren't commanded whom you must love," Father Andrew explained softly. "Not all parents deserve our love when they treat their children in an ill or disrespectful fashion—not in the way Jesus teaches us, certainly. But we still must honor them because they are part of our family. And you can do that by leading a righteous life and bringing honor to your family. Even if your father doesn't understand, your mother would be honored by your admirable actions."

This discussion gave Matty a huge sense of relief. He didn't discuss this with anyone, though. It was something warm he kept buried deep in his heart that he could think about when the bad thoughts threatened his happiness. He promised himself to lead a righteous life that would have pleased his mother, and he would honor her in that way. He lost some of the guilt he had about his feelings toward his father, and he figured he would be a good person in spite of the man. There was no reason to wallow in harsh feelings.

For now, Matty was happy to be safe. And he was happy to be with Nico.

Nighttime was the best. Nico continued to sleep next to Matty in his bed, even though Matty could have moved to a new room. No one questioned their need to stay together.

When the lights were extinguished, the two young men wrapped themselves around each other. They exchanged quiet, vague words of love and promised to always remain steadfast to one another. They would be friends for life. Best friends. Nico's friendly kisses on Matty's shoulder or hands gradually moved to Matty's face, and one night they found each other's mouths at the same time. Open-mouthed gasps gave way to explorative kisses as they sought more and more from one another. Tongues tasted and dueled, probed, and explored. And in doing so, ignited a passion that reached southward in their bodies like an uncontrolled brushfire.

Matty groaned as Nico rubbed against him, and instantly Nico pulled back and stopped. "Did I hurt you?" he asked in a panic. The last thing he wanted was to cause Matty an iota of discomfort.

Matty chuckled. "That wasn't a pained moan, you lunk. I liked what you did and how it felt. Do it some more. If you hurt me, I'll let you know." With a gleam in his eye, he whispered, "You can use your hand if you like."

Nico reached out and cupped Matty through his nightshirt and tentatively began to stroke up and down. His own body felt on fire with need. This was incredible. He loved the feel of Matty in his hand, but something even better happened when Matty snaked his hand beneath Nico's nightshirt and grasped

Nico's cock. Nico felt ready to explode, but the sensation was so magical, he wanted it to last forever. Matty was touching him too… and with his warm, bare hand, skin to skin.

Not to be outdone, Nico gripped Matty's shirt and tugged it up and out of his way. His hand sought and wrapped around Matty's member, and Matty let out a pleased sound that definitely had nothing to do with pain. "Yes!" Matty hissed. "Don't stop."

Nico suddenly wanted to see what was going on and let go long enough to fling back the bedding. In the moonlit room, he delighted with the sight of their two stiff cocks—Matty's surrounded by a thatch of black hair, and his own by a crop of curls a few shades darker blond than the curls on his head. They were both beautiful—the same but different. Nico had the strongest urge to rub his face all over Matty's body, so he shoved Matty's shirt even higher and leaned in to feel his friend with his lips and face. Matty had a clean, musky smell Nico wanted to taste, so he ran his tongue from Matty's sternum, past his navel and into his pubic area. Mindful of his injuries, Nico gently nuzzled Matty with his nose and his lips until Matty begged him for more.

"Please, Nico, Stroke me. I'm about to explode, and I need you."

As Nico settled back and took hold of Matty again, Matty returned the favor, and they mutually rubbed each other with firm grasps until first Matty and then Nico let go and spilled their seed with soft cries of pleasure.

When their breathing slowed, Nico asked, "Are you alright?"

"Never better," Matty replied with a chuckle. "I could do that forever."

"I think my fathers do a lot more than that. I sort of walked in on them and saw… things."

"Really?"

"Yes. When you feel all better, maybe we can try it."

"That sounds good. In the meantime, I loved this." Matty yawned. "I'm sleepy now though."

Nico got up and grabbed a towel to clean them up before climbing back into bed.

The next night Nico added kisses to his exploration of Matty's body and quickly learned how to excite and please Matty with his mouth. He loved the taste of Matty's release. Unfortunately, it was too difficult and painful for Matty to bend over and return the favor with his broken ribs still giving him considerable pain. So they had to become creative, and Nico showed Matty how he could lie in bed while Nico stood next to it. The first time Nico exploded into Matty's mouth in this fashion, he thought he would die from the pleasure. It was also less messy this way, they rationalized.

Without a doubt, they loved each other. And this was how they expressed it night after night… until everything changed.

CHAPTER
Five

It had been about six weeks since Matty moved in, and he felt only moderate pain from his injuries. His face was back to normal without any bruising. The break in his nose had healed, leaving behind only the slightest crook in the shape of his lovely patrician nose. Both of the young men had been studying Walter's, and (in Nico's case) Doc Louis', books, so not being in school didn't matter much. Doc Louis and his elegant Marguerite came to dinner often, and Doc Louis quizzed Nico on what he'd been reading. He always seemed happy with their discussions.

Matty continued his challenging conversations with Father Andrew as well, and he and Nico would discuss what they'd spoken about at dinner after they retired. In this fashion, they were both getting a darn good education in science, history, and philosophy. Their school had not managed to rebuild yet because of continued flooding.

Would this weather *ever* stop? Everyone wondered.

It was during one of their more well-attended dinners that it happened. Since life had been quiet for weeks, the front gate was unlocked to let their guests in, and everyone had their guard down. All of a sudden, the sound of the heavy front door smashing against the wall reverberated through the house and a man's angry voice hollered, "Where is he?! Where is that good-for-nothing?" His footsteps and voice drew nearer and nearer to the dining room.

"Matty, hide under the table!" Nico hissed. But Matty just stared at him. Whether he refused to hide or was simply frozen in terror, Nico couldn't tell.

Isaac, Walter, Royal, Jasper, Doc Louis, and the two other Stark-James sons Bay and Warren jumped to their feet. Actually, Doc Louis didn't exactly jump. He sort of hitched himself upward. He was not about to avoid a fight, even at his age. The men faced the oncoming intruder as a united wall.

Mr. Remington stomped into the room. "Where is that useless son of mine? He's been hiding out here for weeks now, and he needs to come back and take care of business at home!" The crimson-faced man was shaking with anger.

Matty wondered what business he was supposed to be handling as he'd never had to do any such thing in the past other than make sure his father didn't kill him or himself. He also wondered what had triggered this outburst.

Just then, Jeb Hawkins appeared behind the intruder. Jeb's forehead was bleeding copiously into his eye, and Jeb made a smear of it with his hand as he tried to clear his vision.

As shock rippled through the room, Bay took advantage. He whispered to Walter that he was running for the police, and while everyone was staring at a bleeding Jeb, the eldest Stark-James son slipped out of the room and out the front door. Suzette also noticed Bay's escape, but everyone else, including Remington, seemed distracted by Jeb's injuries.

Even as he was nodding in acknowledgement of Bay's whispered words, Walter's eyes never left Jeb's bleeding face. His voice shook as he asked, "What happened to you?"

"This bastard was hiding in the bushes outside. When I turned around, he bashed me with a whiskey bottle and ran for the door before I could get to my feet. He could've taken my eye out!"

Isaac, looking thunderous, bellowed at Remington, "You brutally attack our friend and barge into our house making demands of our houseguest? We'll see what the police have to say about this!"

Remington grinned like a madman and pulled a small gun out of his pocket. He pointed it straight at Isaac's heart and said, "Matty, get up and get out of here. We're going home. *Now!*"

"Don't hurt anyone, Pa. I'm coming." Matty stood as Nico reached for him and grasped his arm. Matty gave Nico a look, shaking his head slightly, and pulled away. "Let's go then. Let everyone get back to their nice dinner. We don't want to interrupt them anymore now, Pa."

Remington's anger flagged a bit seeing his son comply with his demands. His chest puffed out and he got a nasty smirk on his face. "Move!" he barked.

As Matty rounded the table, Remington grabbed him by the arm with his free hand. He kept the gun out where he could brandish it at everyone. As they started to leave, Suzette demanded, "You cannot take Matty out in this storm without a coat! Let me go fetch one for him." She clearly wanted to let Bay get a good head start.

Remington sneered at her. "My son isn't some weakling like you've all been making him out to be. He can make it home in a little rain without harm." With that, he gave Matty a vicious yank.

Matty gasped in pain and stumbled, but knowing his manners, he turned as well as possible toward Suzette and said in as normal a voice as he could muster, "Thank you, ma'am, and all of you, for your hospitality." He then looked at Nico with eyes that penetrated into Nico's very soul. They said what he could not in front of his father. They said, "I love you." Out loud he whispered, "Don't worry." And he was dragged out into the storm by his lunatic father.

Walter turned sharply toward Nico and ordered, "Do *not* think of following them. You could get yourself or Matty shot. The police will take care of this."

About twenty minutes later, Bay returned with two policemen, who were given the complete story of what happened. The police looked grim as the details were recounted. They explained that while it appeared Remington had kidnapped Matty, because the young man was his son, he didn't really. He was definitely guilty of battery on Mr. Hawkins and of brandishing a gun in the Stark-James house, however. The police also acknowledged the possible danger Matty was in being around that man. It was agreed that, at the very least, they would go and speak to Remington. So Isaac and Walter led the police to the Remington house.

Matty opened the door himself and looked mighty relieved to see his friends and the police. He had a swollen, bloody lip. "Thank you for coming. My father is in his study," he said calmly. "He's passed out because he's had too much liquor. Again." He didn't mention that after his father smashed him in the face, Matty had cracked the man over the head with a heavy cigar case when Remington turned away to pour himself a drink. His father lay in a puddle of whiskey and vomit but seemed to be trying to sit up.

"We'll take him to the police station," one of the officers said. He looked at Matty and asked, "Will you be alright here on your own?" Looking around, they could all see that the house was a wreck. Apparently, more of the household staff— if not all—had deserted their posts.

"We'll take care of Matty," Isaac told them quietly. "We have a plan to get him away from this house for good."

Matty had mixed feelings about this announcement. Did

this mean away from Nico too? One half of him felt tremendous relief, and the other half was devastated.

As the police dragged Remington away stumbling, Walter told Matty, "Son, go pack a valise of all your clothes and whatever else you need to have around you for your personal comfort. You're going to take a trip."

"May I please see Nico first?"

"Sorry, no. The less Nico knows for now, the better. We don't want him to have to lie. When things calm down, perhaps you can write to him."

Matty's heart shattered. This did not sound good at all. But at least he'd be away from his father's fists.

Later that night, Walter and Isaac escorted Matty to Father Andrew's house. The priest did not seem surprised in the least to see them.

He nodded and thanked the men and opened his door wide for Matty. "We'll get your face cleaned up tonight, young man. Your train leaves in the morning." He looked at Matty's sad expression and said, "I know it's hard right now, my son. But you are setting out on a grand adventure. Don't look so gloomy."

Matty turned to Walter and Isaac and dropped his valise. He reached out and embraced first Walter and then Isaac, telling them, "Thank you for saving my life and for raising Nico to be such a fine man. I won't ever forget this. The time I spent at your house has been the happiest I've ever been."

Then he turned to Father Andrew and asked, "Will you hear my confession, Father?"

Father Andrew nodded and answered with a sigh, "If you wish to unburden yourself, of course." He looked at Isaac and Walter and said, "Thank you and good night, gentlemen. We'll take it from here."

PART

Two

CHAPTER
Six

Once Nico finally understood that Matty was truly gone, he felt so full of rage, he wanted to rail at the sky and lash out with his fists. The injustice of it all! His beloved friend was ripped from his life, and Nico had no idea how to find him.

Walter had to assure him, "We have no knowledge of Matty's location—only that he is in a safe place and away from his potentially murderous father."

Nico snarled at his fathers until Isaac told him, "You darned well better keep your attitude in check and behave like a gentleman. Your cross words won't bring Matty back. The important thing is that Matty is safe, and his awful father is not likely to find him."

Nico didn't know he'd had it in himself to hate anyone as

much as he detested Mr. Remington, but he relented and answered, "Yes sir. I apologize."

He waited for word from Matty to arrive by mail, but weeks went by, and nothing happened. During this time, Nico begged his parents to find out Matty's whereabouts and eventually went so far as to threaten to leave and look for his friend himself. Suzette, Isaac, and Walter had some serious talks with him about the stupidity of that harebrained notion. He finally had to grudgingly agree.

Months went by. The horrendous rain finally stopped and seemed to be gone for good. The city of Los Angeles went through a long period of cleaning up and rebuilding from flood damage. Nico's school let the students come back to study, but without his friend, Nico was lonely and depressed, and he had to fight against apathy in all his classes without Matty there with him. His fierce anger had finally abated, and it was replaced by a profound sense of sadness.

Remington spent a few weeks in jail after his assaults, but since no one had been seriously injured, his sentence was short. After getting out of jail, he periodically tried to harass Nico for information about Matty's whereabouts. He was certain Nico must know something and was lying to him. The Stark-James family enlisted Jeb Hawkins to act as a bodyguard for Nico when he went from home to school and then to Doc Louis' clinic to work. This managed to keep the horrible man at bay, and they could all stop worrying about Nico's safety.

Nico almost wished Remington would physically attack him so he could pummel the horrible drunkard, but he knew he couldn't use his fists against a gun. So Nico stayed close to Jeb Hawkins—especially since he carried a weapon—and ignored Remington's tirades.

Luckily, Nico's newfound source of education with Doc Louis saved him from losing his mind. He discovered that the medical profession fascinated him far more than anything his school offered, and he was quite good at retaining the information he needed. He had to pay close attention to detail at all times because the well-being of patients was at stake, and that kept his brain occupied. Among other things, Doc Louis showed him how to clean and stitch wounds, set broken bones, treat a fever, and even deliver a baby. At first, Nico simply observed, but eventually Doc Louis entrusted Nico with small tasks that gradually grew in complexity.

Doc Louis was a patient and thorough teacher and continued to provide Nico with interesting reading material to supplement his education. He often quizzed Nico the next day about what he'd given him to read, and that led to some eye-opening ideas. Nico had absolutely no doubt that he'd found his calling and thanked Doc Louis multiple times for giving him such a wonderful opportunity. Doc Louis would simply smile and wave him off.

Often Nico went home after a long shift feeling accomplished and good about his progress—until he crawled into bed. His nights were dismal, and his heart weighed down his chest like a lead weight. He longed for the feel of Matty in his arms, and often hot tears streaked down his face while he tried to get the sleep he badly needed. He was not likely to forget Matty and the love they shared.

He thought over and over of the last night they were together and how Matty had welcomed Nico into his body, promising he was strong enough and knowing Nico would never hurt him. The sheer ecstasy when they were joined together filled Nico with so much love, he thought his heart would burst with it. He could feel his love pouring into Matty and Matty's love expressed in his shuddering climax as they showered each other with affection. Little had they known then that they would so quickly be torn apart. Nico had not even been able to return the favor and allow Matty access to his body in the same fashion. It was the cruelest joke.

He thought the other students in his classes seemed so young and naïve in comparison to Matty and him. He'd never gotten particularly close to anyone else while Matty was there, and without Matty, he retreated even more into his isolation.

TWO YEARS OF HIS LIFE WENT BY IN THIS WAY, AND WHILE THE pain of losing Matty lost some of its sharp edges, it never completely went away. Nico finished his regular studies and accomplished so much with Doc Louis' patients, he felt like he knew nearly everything there was to know—until one day his mentor took him aside and announced, "I have secured you entrance into medical school up in San Francisco where your family and I have many wonderful old friends. You shall be starting next month."

"Medical school?" Nico gasped. "After the procedures I've undertaken with you?" He hardly thought he needed that after what he'd seen and done. He was sure medical school was a superfluity at this point. Surely, he could learn all he needed right here.

And when—or if—Matty ever returned, Nico would be here waiting. How could he leave and go four hundred miles away?

"Ah, please do not be so naïve, Nico, and do not try to cast aside the promise you made about attending medical school because you think you know more than you do. You may want to specialize, become a surgeon, study diseases and how to diagnose them—any number of things. I can only do so much with you. This clinic will be here for you when you return, and with more knowledge you might want to turn it into something unique. I plan to eventually turn it over to you, but only once you have a proper degree—as we agreed originally. You will enjoy it, son, and you will learn of amazing new developments in medicine. Many advancements came about out of necessity during the War Between the States, and you will study them. I may be an old man, but I am not in a hurry." He clapped Nico on the back and said with a smile, "There is also a new school of nursing near the medical school, so before you come home, you should visit them and see if there is a woman you might hire who will travel to Los Angeles and assist you in the clinic."

"Why would I need a woman to help in the clinic?"

"There is a somewhat new way of thinking that a woman named Florence Nightingale began. We already have a couple of schools for women based on her teachings in the east, and now we also have one in San Francisco. There are many women who are interested in the medical profession but know that only men are suited to be doctors. These women learn how to make our patients more comfortable as they recuperate —or as they die. Statistics show their nursing assistance has improved the recovery rate of patients around the world. The key is that they focus on patient hygiene and well-being. I would highly recommend that you meet some of these women and see if anyone suits you. My understanding is that most of them devote themselves to the care of the sick like a nun takes her vows—with complete devotion."

"Why haven't you hired a nurse, Doc Louis?"

He chuckled, "Because I am old and crotchety, and I would probably be mean and bark at anyone who tried to help. And then she would cry, and I would feel remorse, and I do not wish to have that happen." Nico smiled at his friend as Doc Louis continued, "You, however, are still young and need to learn how to run the clinic anyway. You will be able to establish care the way that will suit you, and having help is always good when something is new. Just think about it, Nico.

It is not as if you would have to marry the woman. If having her work for you does not pan out, you can tell her to go find her own sick people." Doc Louis shrugged.

Nico decided he would eventually look into Doc Louis' idea, knowing it would be quite a while before he was ready to come home anyway.

As he prepared to leave for the trip north, he felt confident that his advanced knowledge of medical practices would put him way ahead of anyone else, and he would shine.

However, just as Doc Louis said, Nico had been naïve. When he arrived at school, he discovered that several other would-be doctors had backgrounds similar or even more advanced than his. He fit right in, but he was not some special, superior student. He soon realized that humility was yet another lesson he needed to learn.

For the next couple of years, Nico studied diligently. Doc Louis was correct about everything. Nico was fascinated and challenged and made some interesting friends now that he was among like-minded men. He had not been prepared for the competitive nature of some of his fellow students, however, and was saddened to see young men who were ready to manipulate the truth to get ahead. One young man was finally expelled from the program when his lies were made apparent, and Nico did not miss him in the least. Nico had suspected the man had been inflating his research results, and when his deception went so far overboard it was laughable, that was the end of his medical education at this school.

Nico's career prospects were enviable in his circle of new friends. Taking over an established practice in his hometown sounded wonderful. Some of the men planned to work with their fathers, and others weren't certain at all of what they would be doing—only that doctors were needed everywhere because small towns in the western states were growing. The future of these students was unsettling to Nico, and he wished they had a better outlook for where they would end up.

Now and then, as time allowed, he would take the trek up the hill to see his fathers' former business partners Séamus and Timothy at The Discovery. He met their numerable relatives and friends who'd taken over the running of the hotel when Isaac, Walter, Jasper, and Royal had moved on to their building company. The Irishmen were always great company, and even though San Francisco was a new city for him, he fit right in and belonged. It was a good feeling—especially after his period of terrible depression over losing Matty. Nico admitted to himself that he needed friends, and he'd done himself no favors by distancing himself from his classmates at his school in Los Angeles.

Doc Louis was also correct about the nearby nursing school and its impact on medicine. Feelings were mixed among the doctors who taught Nico and his peers—as well as among the students—as to the appropriateness of women in the medical profession at all. There were several heated debates on the topic. Nico tried to keep an open mind after what Doc Louis had told him. Having help sounded good, but like the other men of his time and education, he had a few doubts. The biggest questions they raised were whether the women were educated enough to be effective and whether they had the stomach for the work. Some men even went so far as to question the moral character of women who might want a career in medicine as the work did not exactly conform to the ideals of a proper Victorian woman. Nico thought that was going a bit far, but he was raised by free-thinking parents who didn't try to conform to much of what was deemed proper by Victorian standards. He kept those opinions to himself, however.

He also kept to himself how he'd been raised. His parents had explained to him that their life was unconventional when they were living in San Francisco, but attitudes there had taken a dramatic shift toward traditional morals once an influx of wives came to join their husbands and churches became popular. Now that he was away from the protective bubble of his family and their closest friends, Nico never brought it up to anyone. Even though he was raised by a mother and two fathers, and their closest friends also lived in the same type of arrangement, no one he met had ever said a word about *their* "two fathers." It wasn't that he felt ashamed in any way, but he didn't want his family examined by strangers and determined to be doing anything wrong or immoral. All he could see was how much they all loved one another. Now and then, a classmate would make a disparaging comment about a stranger's supposed lifestyle, so

Nico kept his mouth shut. These people didn't know his parents, which meant they had no right to judge them. It was safer to remain silent on the topic. He deftly avoided probing questions.

There was a popular café near the medical school that Nico and his classmates favored, and they would often meet up with one another by simply dropping in and sitting with whomever was already there.

One evening, as Nico entered the cafe, he literally bumped into the back of a young lady, startling her and causing her to drop her reticule. He hastily spoke up as he bent to retrieve it for her. "I am so sorry, miss. Please, may I buy you dinner to apologize for my oafishness? I wasn't looking where I was going." He sheepishly held up a pamphlet to show her what had distracted him.

The woman, who was looking for a place to sit, took in the sight of this tall man who appeared close to her age. He had broad shoulders, shiny golden curls, and earnest, deep blue eyes. His friendly smile took her breath away. She agreed to join him for a meal more hastily than she could have ever believed of herself, but this young man exuded brains, charm, and oh—was he ever beautiful to look at.

"Think nothing of it. I'm sorry I was blocking the entrance. But well… yes, thank you, sir," she said, sounding both friendly and educated.

If Nico had friends who were seated already, he was unaware of their presence. He was entranced by this delightful creature. Together, they located the one free table and focused on nothing but each other.

Eden Godwin. Oh, but she was special. She hailed from San Juan Capistrano where her parents had a ranch—not that far from Los Angeles. She first attracted Nico with her wavy black hair and lovely light blue eyes—a combination that reminded him immediately of Matty. But she was all female with luscious curves. She smelled like flowers and had a sweet, soft voice that soothed Nico. He could listen to her talk about… well… just about anything. Her laugh resonated in his chest and made him swell with desire for her. For the first time since being with Matty, he felt attraction to another person, and also for the first time in years, he felt that profound sadness in his heart recede a bit. Her very presence eased his angst.

Discovering that she was not a San Franciscan, Nico asked, "What brings you to this city?"

"I came up here to study at the nursing school, actually. I've been here for several months now. It can be interesting work, but I am not at all certain that the profession is truly my calling now that I've given it a try."

"May I ask why you wanted to do it in the first place and why you are considering quitting?"

Eden cocked her head to the side and set down her utensils. She paused so long before answering him, he wasn't sure she was going to. Finally, she answered stiffly, "I knew I didn't want to be a rancher's wife like my mother, and the opportunity to dedicate myself to helping people sounded… well… noble, I suppose. Our property is terribly secluded, and I had little interaction with anyone other than my family, so I begged to be sent away to school. I heard about the nursing program opening up, and that sounded practical. Now that I'm here, I find that the other women in the program all take to it like it's a religious calling, and they cannot conceive of doing anything else or being anything else. Many of them have expressed that they never intend to marry or set down roots anywhere—they plan to devote everything to their vocation. While I admire their devotion, I can't find that level of commitment within myself. I truly hope this doesn't make me sound selfish or uncaring—because I *do* care. I began the studies with every intention of becoming a nurse to help the sick and the wounded. It sounded so perfect, but sometimes I wonder if I am missing the level of dedication I really need for the job. I've lain awake night after night second-guessing my decision to stay and continue with the program when—if I'm honest with myself—in my heart, I do want to marry a nice man and raise a family. However, I'm afraid my parents will be upset after they agreed to send me up here to study, and now I have decided I want what they wanted for me all along. I just don't want it to be on a cattle ranch." Eden did not add that she suspected her parents were merely humoring her temporarily and expected her to come home and marry a man they'd picked out for her. This thought was a horrible one considering the man they probably wanted her to marry. She looked down and then back up at him. "Does that make you think I am a shallow, selfish person?"

"No. Not in the least. You are being honest with what you want, and not everyone is cut out for that kind of profession. I see nothing wrong with you questioning yourself. It also takes dedication and commitment to raise a family, no matter where you live. My mother raised five children, and I'm certain we provided her with plenty of challenging moments." He laughed but didn't add that his mother had help from two dedicated husbands.

Eden's stiff shoulders relaxed, and she gave him a grateful smile. "I don't know why I felt so compelled to unburden myself on you this way since you are a virtual stranger. I haven't told a single other person about my doubts." She noticed his patient smile and continued, "Enough about me and my worries, what are *you* doing in San Francisco?"

One side of Nico's mouth raised in a mildly sardonic grin, and he answered, "I'm here studying medicine." He chuckled softly when he saw Eden flinch. "I only have a few months left before earning my degree, and then I plan to return to Los Angeles to take over a friend's clinic when he retires. I worked there for a couple of years before starting medical school here. Unlike you, I *can't* conceive of any other career."

"Oh. Lucky for you."

"Yes, I am lucky in many ways, and I need to remember that more often, I suppose." He paused for a moment and then spoke with resolve. "I am also fortunate that for a man, a career in medicine does not preclude getting married and raising a family as long as he can find a suitable partner who is amenable to him keeping long and irregular hours at work some of the time."

"Why do you say you need to remember that you're lucky?"

Now it was Nico's turn to reflect on how much to tell this lovely woman. He looked away at nothing and then back at her with an earnest expression. "I have always lived in comfort. My family has been extremely successful, and they all love one another as well as their circle of friends fiercely. I have been given an excellent education and an even better opportunity for my vocation when I return to Los Angeles." His eyes suddenly looked sad. "I have, however, experienced a great sorrow that I find challenging to get past. I have much to be grateful for. But the loss I experienced has left me with a sense of anguish I need to subdue. I guess I feel somewhat betrayed, and that is difficult for me to get beyond."

"I see." She didn't really. Eden thought at first that someone close to him had died until he spoke of betrayal, and now she wasn't certain. She was beginning to think he'd been jilted by a lover, though she couldn't conceive of any woman turning away from this man. "Do you want to talk about it? I can be a good listener."

"Thank you for the offer, but no. Not even a little. I will try to focus on the blessings of my life and forget the loss. What's done is done, and I need to look forward." Nico gave

Eden a bright smile then and asked, "May I see you again after tonight? You're not planning to leave San Francisco soon, are you?"

"Oh, no. I don't have any immediate plans to leave, and I would be delighted to see you again, Nico. Maybe together we can make you forget your sadness."

That sounded promising to him, and it made something inside rise to attention. So, after they finished their meal, Nico placed her hand in the crook of his arm and escorted her back to the women's dormitory. "I had a wonderful time meeting you, Eden. Would you like to do some sightseeing and have dinner with me this Saturday?"

"Why yes, thank you."

Over the next weeks, Eden's interest in her nursing program didn't change, but now that Nico presented her with another reason to stay in San Francisco, she felt less despair. Keeping company with him was infinitely better than returning home and being married off to a rancher. As her training continued, Eden also lost some of her previously unadmitted disgust over blood and bedpans, and she sympathetically acknowledged the loss of privacy and propriety her patients had to endure. This helped her want to care for them more than ever before. Now that she had a friend—a handsome, attentive friend at that—she felt better about her life and also accepted the zealous fellow students with more understanding. She wanted to help patients and saw the positive results of her care, though she still wasn't completely sure it was her ultimate calling.

Eden and Nico saw each other several times over dinner and even managed a night out once to enjoy an amusing local theater production. Nico felt a growing calm in himself that took up the black void that had previously filled his heart. He thought Eden was beautiful and charming, and he asked her often how her studies were going. Whenever she smiled and told him things were going well, it pleased him greatly. He was formulating a plan. Walking her back to the dormitory after dinner one night, he broached it with her.

Remembering Doc Louis' advice, he asked, "Eden, I'd love nothing more than to take you back to Los Angeles where you can work alongside me in the clinic. Will you marry me?" He could have been a lot more romantic about this, but he felt it was a practical solution, and he was terribly fond of her. He just knew she would jump at the chance. Eden could help people *and* have a husband, and he could provide that life for her.

Eden was not so easily swept off her feet by the promise of a job. Her brow furrowed as she tried to smile at him. "Thank you, Nico. I… um… I'm not sure we're ready for that. Do you even love me?" Even though he had advanced to chaste goodnight kisses that held a bit of promise, he'd never mentioned any feelings he had for her.

Nico's jaw dropped. He hadn't considered that she would

have any hesitation because he was pretty sure she loved him. "I… well… I suppose I do love you, Eden."

"Then ask me again when you're *sure*." She smiled and kissed him lightly. "I'm not going anywhere, but I want you to be certain. Sometimes I think there are other things on your mind when we're together. I get this odd sensation that you're speaking as if to someone else and not always to me. Or maybe you *wish* you were speaking to someone else…" It was time to get it out of him, so she asked, "Did someone hurt you in the past?" Maybe she could get to the bottom of his reluctance to show more than superficial affection.

An icy frost trickled down Nico's spine. *Am I that transparent?* "I… yes, I suppose so. Not someone I wish to speak of, but someone I need to forget."

Nodding calmly, Eden repeated, "I see. I'm sorry you were hurt, but ask me again when you're truly ready, Nico. I won't be a substitution. *I* need to be the most important person to you if we are to ever marry. And you can then expect the same of me. As for the job offer you present, I don't know if I can accept that without understanding what I mean to you."

Nico covered his mild confusion about her rebuff with a polite smile and resolved to make Eden his priority. He would study hard and become the best doctor he could be, and he would treat her with the utmost kindness and respect, giving her his full attention when he wasn't working. He promised himself that he would love her the way she deserved.

It almost worked.

CHAPTER
Seven

During the weeks that followed, Nico tried to be as affectionate with Eden as possible and poured his feelings into his words and his kisses—even if they were generally delivered at the doorstep of her dormitory. He was delighted when Eden responded to him with enthusiasm. Sadly for both of them, however, he had cases and exams and all manner of distractions piled onto him as they neared the end of his term, so their available time to spend together was limited.

Over and over, Nico found himself apologizing to Eden for not being able to dine with her or take a walk and relax after a long day. But the fact that he missed her so much when he couldn't be around her solidified his thinking that he truly did love her. He reasoned with himself that he needed her in his life, and he had to do a much better job of convincing her. She seemed to understand, but he still wanted to prove to her that she was a priority in his life. When they didn't have the opportunity to see each other for a few days, he would dispatch notes to her, pouring his heart out on paper. When he could, he would bring her small bouquets of flowers, and one time he gave her a lovely copy of Walt Whitman's *Leaves of Grass*. She was quite touched by his thoughtfulness, so he counted that as progress.

Finally, when he had a weekend off coming up, he asked her if she would consider having a special night with him. "I have old family friends who own a wonderful hotel here in San Francisco that my fath… uh… family helped build. It's called The Discovery. They've urged me to come up and visit them more often. We can have dinner with them and, if you would like, we can also get a room for the night."

When Eden wasn't rapidly forthcoming with her answer, Nico decided to make his point more clearly. Looking deeply into her eyes, he said, "I'm sorry, my dearest. I don't mean to be putting the cart before the horse. I just want to show you in the best way possible how much you mean to me and how deeply I have fallen in love with you. If you think this is improper of me, I apologize, but I am dying to make love to you. Should you simply prefer to spend time together, I will understand, but I would love to at least be alone with you for a change. I don't see how we are to accomplish this with our communal living arrangements, so that is why I'm suggesting a private room."

Eden studied his expression to gauge his sincerity and

could see no hesitation or uncertainty in his eyes this time. Because she had been bursting with desire for weeks, she answered, "It's fine, Nico. I would love to go to The Discovery with you." Her insides did a crazy flip as soon as she spoke the words, and she thought to herself, *I hope I'm not making a huge mistake, but I truly love this man.*

That Saturday night, they had a rollicking good time over dinner with Séamus and Timothy and their lovely Irish wives, children, and a couple of grandchildren. Although she greatly enjoyed the laughter and occasional snatches of song, Eden was puzzled by some of the conversation. She was never sure whom they were speaking about when they talked to Nico about someone named Isaac and someone named Walter. One of them was apparently his father, but she was never certain which man it was. No one noticed her confusion as the wine and whiskey flowed freely along with a delicious meal. She finally decided her mystification was because she couldn't understand their Irish accents very well.

Eden answered plenty of questions about living on a cattle ranch and what nursing school was like. She tried to remain positive about both experiences as much as possible. Whenever she could, she deflected the questions and ended up getting a good education about emigrating from Ireland to California. Like Nico, Eden was a native Californian, and her family had settled there from Minnesota in search of a warmer climate. They changed their family business from lumber to cattle when they got to the west coast, and their lack of experience made a hard life even more challenging. At least by the time Eden was born, they were fairly well established. Eden was relieved she had three older brothers to carry on the ranching business. She was the only daughter.

Throughout the meal, she had a growing trepidation about the coming events of the evening, especially when Séamus announced, "It was only fitting that we've given you the suite Walter and Isaac lived in before they moved out and became gentlemen firefighters." Then he laughed and smacked Nico on the back. "We have electricity and indoor plumbing now though, just as Walter always wanted. We're a right modern hotel now, we are."

The suite had obviously been updated in the last twenty or so years. It was a lovely room with a large bed and a sitting area featuring a fireplace that glowed with comforting warmth. The moment the door closed behind them, Nico took Eden into his arms and kissed her. He pulled back and said, "If you have any second thoughts about this, I understand. I'm just so anxious to prove to you my love, but before that happens, I have something important to say." Nico then dropped to one knee and wisely pulled a ring from his pocket this time, saying, "Eden Godwin, my dearest, I love you deeply. I need you in my life forever, and I cannot foresee a future that does not include you. Will you be my wife and the mother of my children?"

Eden smiled, and happy tears glistened in her eyes as she

answered, "Yes, Nico, I'll marry you." That was the kind of proposal she'd been hoping for.

Slipping the ring onto her finger, he said, "You are making me the happiest man in all of California. I promise to love you and cherish you forever. If you choose to work in the clinic or not is completely up to you. I love you and want you no matter what your decision is." He rose to his feet and kissed her gently and sweetly. Then less gently and less sweetly—more wildly and possessively. His hand stroked over one breast as he splayed the other over her buttock through her clothing. All he could feel was a lot of material, and that wouldn't do. He pulled back and looked for clues as to how to get Eden out of her pretty dress. "I think I need some assistance here," he admitted. "I've never undressed a woman."

"Ah, so you are as new to this as I am? Somehow that's a bit comforting."

Nico paused for a split second and answered truthfully, "I have never lain with a woman. You will be the first. I am not, however, uneducated as to how this works." Nico felt a twinge of guilt for being misleading about his lack of virginity, but the last thing he wanted to think about was his experience with Matty. This night was all about Eden and expressing his love for her.

She laughed softly and nodded. "Mm hmm… medical books. I've read my share as well."

"I also want to reassure you that I have a prophylactic to use in case you're worried about becoming pregnant."

"That's quite thoughtful of you, Nico." She smiled and kissed him again and began to undo her clothes. Nico stood spellbound as each article of clothing revealed a little more of this enchanting creature. "Darling," she said, "please get your clothes off as well. I'm beginning to feel all alone in my state of undress, and it's a tad embarrassing."

Nico couldn't take his eyes off of her as she got down to her thin undergarments. He'd seen every part of a woman while examining them and delivering babies, of course, but this was completely different. This was beautiful in a delightful new way that aroused him to his very core. Quickly, he began to divest himself of his jacket and pants, relieved when he could decrease the pressure threatening to choke his manhood. He couldn't stop staring at her, though, and wanted to feel every inch of her body when it was at last revealed to him. Her breasts were pert and round with rosy nipples, and he suddenly had the urge to taste them. Her waist was thin and the curve of her hips alluring. He whipped off his last article of clothing and reached for her, sighing when their bodies fit together perfectly. His proud cock rubbed against her belly, sandwiched between them as they embraced, and the feel of her warm, silky skin against him was perfect.

"Mm, husband-to-be, I've never seen a naked man in a state of arousal before, and I must say, it's quite impressive."

He glowed with pride and nuzzled her neck. "It's all because of you."

Eden stepped back and took him by the hand as she led him to the bed saying, "Nico, my dearest, I need you now."

Nico felt an almost overpowering rush of desire. He bent over to retrieve a discreet tin box from the pocket of his now-discarded trousers. He placed the box on the bedside table and then turned down the covers and lowered the lights. The room was finally only illuminated by the glowing fireplace and the moonlight filtering through the curtains.

They both climbed into bed and reached for each other. They kissed and kissed as their hands roamed over each other's bodies. Nico was one hundred percent aware that he was with Eden, but as he reached between her legs the first time and felt the soft patch of hair and not much else, he had a momentary mental hiccup—as if something was missing. Then, he drove his hand lower and deeper until an enticing warmth and wetness coated his fingers. Eden let out a sigh of pleasure, and he tried to banish the remembrance of anything else he'd done with another lover. She was to be his wife. He loved her. He had to remember only that… not… the other.

He did remember the pleasure he'd both given and received with lips and tongues, however, and decided to try an experiment. He kissed down Eden's neck to her breasts and toyed with them a while, licking and pulling with his lips. Her gasps and moans made him feel a hundred feet tall. So, he continued to explore lower and lower on her body until she whispered, "Nico! Oh my gracious! That's… oh!"

Nico spread her legs and raised her knees. He chuckled

and decided he was on the right path as he explored her with his tongue. He found a slightly stiff spot that when he stroked elicited a deep moan from Eden. He'd read about this part of a woman and the importance of it, and the books did not lie. Eden was delighted with his ministrations. Deciding to go all in, he nibbled lightly on this little nub and then sucked it into his mouth. Eden's body lurched and she made an unholy sound of surprise.

Pulling away, he asked, "Did I hurt you? That wasn't my intent at all!"

Eden laughed and demanded, "No! Do that some more. It was incredible." To accent her point, she threaded her fingers into his hair and firmly encouraged his head back into position.

So, aiming to please, he dove right back in and sucked that little pleasure button into his mouth again. Only this time, he added his finger as he slid it into her slippery, hot body. He stroked in and out a few times, sensing that Eden was tensing up. Wanting to relax her, he doubled his efforts and sucked harder until she nearly screamed, "Nico!" Her body spasmed over and over as Nico went from sucking back to gently licking her.

He felt victorious. He understood *that* reaction.

"I've never experienced anything like that," she panted incredulously. "It was like a fierce grip of pleasure overtook me and lifted me right out of myself."

"You are so beautiful like this, my dearest. All warm and

satisfied. Are you ready for me? I'm afraid what is coming might not feel as wonderful at first, but it's supposed to get better the more you do it." Then he thoughtfully added, "I love you, Eden."

"I love you too. I'm ready."

"Are you sure? Because we can wait if you need me to." He thought he would possibly die on the spot if she said she wasn't ready.

"Nico, are you stalling?" She laughed softly. "Make love to me."

That was enough to convince him, so Nico retrieved his condom from the box on the table, and Eden watched with interest as he carefully covered himself with it. The rubber felt strange, but it was what he'd been taught to prescribe to people who wanted to avoid pregnancy—despite the largely ignored Comstock Act that made them against the law. As much as the idea of being a father filled him with happiness, he was sure they weren't ready for that. Once he was all encased—like he'd pulled a rain boot over his cock—he went back to probing Eden's beautiful body. He could feel how tight a grasp she had on just one finger and wondered how he was ever supposed to fit his cock in there. "Can you relax a bit?"

"I'll try, but maybe you need to try two fingers." She had done her reading too, after all.

Nico nodded at the sage advice. He pulled out and carefully slipped two fingers into her. There was definitely more resistance, so he stroked in and out several times, murmuring soft words of love to her.

"Go ahead, Nico. I know it's going to hurt my first time. I'm not naïve. Let's get it over with so we can get to the enjoyable part."

With that encouragement, Nico positioned himself over her body and lined himself up. Gently, gently, he probed her entrance and retreated. He kissed her and tried again. He pushed in a miniscule amount and pulled out again. Over and over he did this, not making the slightest amount of progress, until Eden wrapped her legs around Nico's, grabbed him by the hips, and shoved herself upward as he started his forward motion one more time. He was forced into her body with the power of Eden's massive thrust as she gasped with an enormous intake of breath. "There!" she cried and laughed at his surprised expression. "Well, one of us had to do it!"

He buried his face in her neck and chuckled, saying, "I love you so much, you wild woman." And with that, he began to pull out and push back in rhythmically. Eden made appreciative noises, and he felt… not much. He knew she was tight, but the fabulous sensation of being inside her was a disappointment—certainly nothing like what he'd experienced with… someone he didn't want to think about at this moment. He decided he needed to move more to make things interesting, so he sped up his efforts and felt Eden's body tighten around him even more. He gave a mighty shove into her, and on the way back out again, the feeling changed, and it became incredibly sensual. That was what he'd expected all along! His cock grew ultra-sensitive to each movement, and he could feel that familiar sensation building and building until he erupted into her silky warmth. Glory, hallelujah, it was transformative! He groaned and collapsed onto her, kissing her neck and then her lips.

But… when he pulled away and reached down to remove the condom, he got red in the face and said, "Whoops. Oh no."

"What could possibly be the matter, Nico? That was wonderful, and it barely hurt at all."

"I lost the condom inside you. It came off. I'm so terribly sorry, Eden."

She blinked and sat up. "Is it going to get lost in there?"

"What? Oh, no. I can get it out again. Don't worry. It's just that the condom didn't do its job very well. I spilled inside you without the protective barrier in place."

"Oh. I see."

Nico reached over and turned the lamp on to get some better light and then asked Eden, "Turn sideways so that you're facing the light and I'll pull it out. I'm so sorry."

"I'm sure it's not your fault," she said as she slid into position, her face turning a bright shade of pink.

He handed her a pillow for her head, and asked her in a somewhat business-like tone, "Please raise your knees and open your legs. A little more, please. Yes, that's right." Nico again slipped two fingers into her, trying to think of this as a medical procedure. It wasn't working. He was becoming aroused again. He knew intimately how wonderful it felt to be inside her, and he could smell her light perfume and musky personal scent. It made him want to bury his face in her again. And it certainly didn't help that Eden was making happy little noises when his fingers moved in and out.

Fishing around inside of her, he noticed the small amount of blood on his hand from her hymen. At least the pain hadn't been too bad, he rationalized. Or maybe she was just stoic. In any case, he finally found the edge of something he could grasp with two fingers and pulled. The vulcanized rubber condom was shredded and liberally coated with semen. It had lost its shape completely and obviously came off as soon as his thrusting had become vigorous. He knew exactly when that happened and why the sensation went from practically nothing to heavenly.

Holding it up where Eden could see it, he tried to make a joke, "Now I see why they're illegal. They don't do the job very well. At least no one in California pays any attention to the Comstock Act. Some states, like Connecticut, aren't as free-thinking about the matter of birth control measures. Anyway, just relax there a moment, and I'll take care of you. No need to get up." Nico disposed of the ruined rubber and washed himself, then he returned with a damp cloth and carefully cleaned Eden with it. "I don't know what's normal in this situation, but you don't seem to have bled much. Are you in any pain?"

"No, I'm a tiny bit tender, but there isn't truly any pain. I can't wait for more of that, to be completely honest." Then she looked into Nico's eyes and asked, "Did I please you?"

"Oh, Eden, you were… you *are* wonderful, my dearest. I'm so glad we came here to spend this time together and that you've agreed to marry me. I can't imagine being any happier." Something in the back of Nico's mind shook a finger at him and called him a liar, saying, *You know what would make you happier… if you had Eden* and *Matty like your parents' arrangement. Then life would be perfect*! He tried to squelch that voice by railing at it that *Eden* was his future, and he was happy *now*. He didn't have to be like his parents to have a good life.

Still…

Nico recognized the time they spent at The Discovery provided a great opportunity to unburden himself and let Eden know more about his background—both regarding his family and Matty. But the time with her seemed too precious to disturb with potentially difficult subjects. When they left the hotel, Nico was both relieved he'd remained silent and furious with himself about it.

CHAPTER
Eight

Nico and Eden had a busy final month as their school programs drew to a close, so they never had a chance to stay overnight at The Discovery again, as much as they both wanted to. Nico knew he'd miss his Irish friends when they headed back to Los Angeles, so he managed to drop in on them one last time to give them a proper goodbye and extend an open invitation to anyone visiting the southern part of the state.

Walter had gotten his way finally and had a telephone installed at the house in Los Angeles, so as Nico's time in medical school drew to an end, he was able to call home to let his family know his plans. As it happened, his mother answered his call, and they ended up speaking in French. Nico was relieved for the added privacy this allowed him, should another student or faculty member wander past or need to use the telephone.

"Maman!" he said happily. "I'm almost all done here, and I'll be home next week."

"Marvelous, Nico. We cannot wait to see you again. How is the end of school going?" They had been in contact by letters and more recently the occasional telephone call, so she knew he loved it there.

"Quite well. I need to tell you and my fathers something important. I'll be bringing my future bride with me."

Suzette gasped. "Nico! You never said a word! Who is she? What is she like?"

With a big smile, Nico explained, "I met her by accident actually, but she is a nursing student—a very lovely one I might add, and I think you're going to love her. Her name is Eden Godwin, and she will travel with me to Los Angeles. I will let you all get acquainted with her, and then we need to see her family at their ranch down near San Juan Capistrano. We will be making our wedding plans when we get there. I suppose I ought to speak to her father as well."

"You would prefer to get married in Capistrano instead of where you will live?"

"Oh, I don't care, Maman. I'll leave that up to Eden. I'm sorry, I have to rush off now because of a paper I need to deliver. Eden and I will be taking the night train, and we'll be home next Tuesday. I'm so anxious to see you, Maman. I love you."

"I love you too, Nico, and I am looking forward to meeting your bride. We'll make sure someone will be at the railroad station to get you. Safe travels."

As their departure day drew nearer, Nico's nerves started to get the best of him. He worried about what it would be like to eventually run the clinic himself, and he had to laugh at his own arrogance for previously thinking he could skip going to medical school before undertaking that job. He also wondered how it would be to be married to Eden. She was so lovely and bright. He loved her curiosity and her fearlessness. She had proved to him on the one night they spent together that she was an adventurous and passionate lover. But he was plagued by a tiny doubt in the back of his mind that she would not be enough for him. He never voiced his concerns to anyone, of course. He thought possibly the only person he might consider speaking to about it was his papa. Of his three parents, he felt the closest understanding with Walter. Nico resolved to speak to him before saying, "I do." He supposed he owed it to Eden and wondered if he should even tell her about Matty. If he should, he was not eager to do it. Telling Eden about having three parents also gave him pause. He didn't think she would refuse him because of that, but so far, he'd been too nervous about it to speak up. He fervently hoped she wouldn't be appalled.

He had so much on his mind, it was staggering, and he still had to make it through the rest of his studies successfully.

Ultimately, Eden agreed to work in the clinic after they

were married because she didn't want to waste her education, and she knew Nico could benefit from her help. She wanted to spend a little time with her family when they arrived in the southern part of the state, but she was not the least bit interested in staying in Capistrano long-term. They would be close enough to visit now and then, and that pleased her. She loved her family, just not ranch life. When Nico finally asked her what it was she disliked so much, she went into a detailed description of castrating male calves, branding livestock, and preparing meals for an ever-changing (large) number of ranch hands. And dirt. Endless dirt. She wanted a life that would stimulate her brain. He understood after that.

Nico discovered he was sad to leave some of his fellow students, and he collected addresses so they could keep in touch once they went their separate ways. He'd become especially close to one fellow named Otto Schubert who came from Idaho and who did not seem all that interested in leaving California to go home. Nico tucked that information away for future reference in case running the clinic became more than he could handle once Doc Louis retired for good.

After a weekend of celebrating with their friends and packing their belongings, Nico and Eden boarded the train and headed south. Nico was able to secure a private compartment for them which was a relief since it was a night train. Eden discovered she was not only exhausted by the time the train took off, she was also queasy from the motion of the train. Nico had looked forward to having several uninterrupted hours with Eden during which they could talk about anything and everything, but she fell asleep almost right away and slept for twelve of the fourteen-hour trip. Eden looked so peaceful sleeping, he didn't have the heart to wake her so she could listen to him unburden himself about his family dynamics.

Nico, on the other hand, was terribly restless. He only managed a couple of short naps, and when he was not resting, he immersed himself in a particularly revolutionary how-to manual called *Modern Methods of Antiseptic Wound Treatment* published by Johnson & Johnson. He had to scoff a little at how everyone thought it was so earth-shattering to keep things sterile—Doc Louis had been stressing cleanliness in the clinic for as long as Nico could remember. The idea of invisible germs creating havoc with infection was extraordinary, however. He absolutely planned to emphasize the practice of sterilizing equipment after reading this.

When he finished his reading, he wished he could sleep too, but his mind was racing about his future.

As soon as the train stopped, Nico caught sight of Walter standing on the platform and waving wildly at him with a grin that looked like it might split his face in two. Nico cried out delightedly, "Papa!" He wanted desperately to rush into his father's arms and hug him close, but he had to help Eden off the train. She still looked a little peaked after the long trip.

Apparently, Walter felt the same overwhelming need for a hug. He dashed toward them and wrapped Nico in his arms, bestowing a kiss on his cheek, exclaiming, "Welcome home, my wonderful, brilliant son the *doctor*. It's so good to have you back at last. We've missed you ferociously!"

Eden tucked that information away, deciding that cleared up her question about Nico's parentage, until Walter continued, "Your mother and father are beside themselves with excitement and wanted to join me, but we wanted to make sure we had room in the carriage for you and your baggage." Then Walter turned and also wrapped Eden in a bear hug, exclaiming, "Welcome to our family, my dear. I'm Nicolo's father Walter James." Now she was terribly confused and tried to smile through her befuddlement. Walter just kept chattering away, not seeming to notice her puzzled expression.

She managed to say, "Pleased to meet you, Mr. James."

Walter laughed and said, "Oh, no. That won't do. Call me Walter, or better yet, Papa, the way Nicolo does. We'll be related soon enough, I understand. And I must say, we're all delighted that you have captured our boy's heart, Eden." He winked at Nico and whispered, "She's quite beautiful, son."

Nico noticed Eden's expression and, as Walter hoisted a valise into the carriage exclaiming proudly that it was so heavy it must contain several wonderful books, Nico whispered to her, "Apparently, I have some explaining to do. Sorry."

Nico did not have a chance to tell her anything on the ride home, however, because Walter took it upon himself to point out all the new buildings and local changes that had happened in Nico's absence. Acting as an enthusiastic Los Angeles ambassador, Walter jabbered on cheerfully and incessantly until they reached the house. Upon their arrival, he turned the carriage over to a stable hand and helped Nico take their bags to the front door where a couple of servants whisked them away.

When they entered the house, a raucous cheer went up,

and a beautiful blonde woman with golden curls similar to Nico's—only hers were interspersed with silver—rushed forward and planted a kiss on both of Nico's cheeks as she clasped him in her arms. She had tears in her eyes, she was so happy to see him, but she was speaking in rapid French, so Eden didn't have any idea what the woman was saying. Finally, the lady stepped back and excused herself to Eden, "Pardon me, my dear, I sometimes get carried away and forget my English, even after all these years. Welcome to our family —I am so thrilled to meet you." Then she bestowed kisses on both of Eden's cheeks as well.

The room was suddenly flooded with a myriad of people who loved and cared for Nico. He was hugged and kissed over and over, first by a man he introduced as his pa, Isaac, and then his brothers Bay and Warren as well as his sisters Ondine and Martha and all of their respective spouses. He had new little nieces and nephews to admire, and there were business associates, friends, employees, and on and on. Obviously, his family was well loved by many, and Nico's achievement was something for everyone to celebrate.

Each time someone approached them to welcome Eden and congratulate Nico, Eden could not help noticing that Nico was polite and cheerful, but he seemed to be looking over a lot of shoulders as if trying to find someone else. This happened over and over until each friend or relative had spoken to them. Nico perused the room one more time, and the light went out of his eyes a bit as his shoulders drooped with a touch of sadness. She wondered just who was missing that would cause such a reaction in him—especially since it felt as if half of Los Angeles was already present. After greeting Nico, most of the non-related guests gradually drifted out to get back to work or get back to their children at home, and it was just Nico's immediate family left with a few others.

She forgot to worry about Nico's melancholy expression, however, when she met Louis Montrachet—the man everyone called Doc Louis—who entered the room briskly despite his age. Eden recognized his name, of course—he had come up multiple times during her courtship with Nico.

Doc Louis was older than anyone else she'd met that day, but he looked sharp and spry despite his thinning white hair. Eden liked him immediately.

The doctor apologized for arriving late, saying he was held up by a broken arm he needed to set. In a heavy French accent he explained, "The imbécile tumbled off his horse last night after too much whiskey, and he did not know it was hurt so badly until he woke up sober this morning."

Doc Louis beamed at Nico as brightly as Nico's family. After speaking to them, Doc Louis wandered off and wrapped his arm around a stylish older French woman named Marguerite she'd met earlier. Eden assumed this was Doc Louis' wife. Marguerite seemed to be close friends with Nico's mother.

At last, Suzette announced, "I'm sure you're both

famished after your long trip, so we'll get you settled in Nicolo's room and then sit down for a nice luncheon."

Eden blinked. "Nico's room?"

"Do you prefer your own room instead?" Suzette asked with a tiny frown. "I do not mean to be presumptuous—I just assumed. But we have plenty of vacant bedrooms."

Eden glanced around and realized the house was enormous. She was momentarily too embarrassed to speak about where she preferred to sleep, however.

Nico broke into her reverie saying, "You presumed just fine, Maman. We'll share my room." Eden's attention snapped to him, and her jaw dropped a little.

"Eh, bien." Suzette gave Eden a sweet smile. "Nicolo must have explained that we are open-minded people in this family. And you are soon to be married, after all." Suzette scrutinized Eden's face, and, noticing her pallor, added, "Quite soon, I assume. Are you feeling well?"

"I, um, well, the train ride was a bit difficult on my stomach, I'm afraid, but I'm frankly quite hungry, so luncheon sounds wonderful, Mrs.… um… *James*...?"

"It's Suzette Stark-James, actually, the same as Nicolo's surname, but please call me Maman. Or, if that makes you uncomfortable, call me Suzette." Looking down at Eden's body with a quick glance, she added, "And may I offer you my congratulations."

"Thank you. We haven't actually set a wedding date yet," Eden replied.

"I understand, but I meant—"

Just then, Walter arrived at her side, producing a tray of champagne glasses, interrupting her with, "Nicolo's graduation from medical school warrants a toast!"

Nico beamed at him and answered with gusto, "Thank you, Papa," as he picked up a glass and handed it to Eden. Then he took one for himself.

Isaac also approached and lifted a glass, saying, "Congratulations to our wonderful son and soon-to-be daughter-in-law. We commend you both for your hard work in school and are delighted with your upcoming marriage."

Walter added hastily, "And may there be many babies! I just love grandchildren. They make us feel young again, don't they, Isaac?" Isaac chuckled at him with fondness, and then he put his arm around Walter to give him a hug that Walter acknowledged with a quick kiss on the cheek.

"À votre santé!" Suzette added and glanced once more at Eden's waistline.

Eden and Nico beamed at each other and swallowed some champagne, then Nico said, "Let me show you to our bedroom, and we'll come back in a few minutes to eat." He looked at Suzette and said, "Thank you, Maman," then at his fathers, one after the other and added, "Pa. Papa. It was so nice of you to have everyone come over to greet us. It was a wonderful homecoming." He took Eden's arm. "Shall we?" He led her down the hall away from his parents. He couldn't help but notice that Eden looked exhausted, and he knew she was famished.

"The luncheon will be served in ten minutes, Nicolo," Suzette called as she headed to the kitchen to make sure everything was ready.

Nico opened the bedroom door and a wave of nostalgia swept over him. Before leaving for San Francisco, this had been his personal domain for his entire life—only ever shared with Matty. He rallied his flagging spirits and said with slightly forced satisfaction, "Oh, look at this, they already put our bags in here for us."

Eden stepped in and realized the room was large and well-appointed with stylish furniture. She'd never had such a lovely space to live in in her life. "This is beautiful, Nico."

That bolstered his spirits because of the pride he felt for Isaac. "My pa made all of the furniture. He's so talented. He's also a violinist. Wait until you hear him and Maman play together. They're incredible."

"Does your papa play too?"

"No. He's like me. Good at other things. He loves books and designs wonderful buildings and sometimes machinery. He probably designed some of the buildings he pointed out on the way here, but he was too modest to say so. He's quite brilliant."

"Excuse me for asking, but which of them is your father?"

"Don't know for sure, but I'm betting on Papa. Walter. Mostly because of my lack of musical talent."

"And your pa doesn't care?"

"Why would he?"

"Well, who is married to your mother?"

"Oh, both of them, I guess."

"You guess?"

"Yes, I'm sorry I never explained this to you. As they tell it, some greedy, shifty judge up in San Francisco married their business partners Royal and Jasper to the lady named Adeline you met earlier. She's also an incredible pianist, by the way, and is one of Pa's—Isaac's—best friends because they've played together for years. I mean music. They've played music." Nico's face turned a little pink. "Anyway, the three of them recommended to Papa, Pa, and Maman that they go find the same judge and get hitched the same way by paying him off with gold. So, I guess they did. My fathers consider themselves married to each other the same as to Maman. It's always seemed normal to me because I was raised around these two families, but when I got to know other kids at school, I realized we were something of an oddity in Los Angeles. Still, no one seems to care much. I hope it doesn't bother you for any reason." He took Eden's hand and looked into her eyes. "If my unconventional family is too much for you, I'll understand. I'd be terribly sad, but I'll understand."

Eden blinked a few times and swayed on her feet a little. "I'm going to be sick," she whispered. Nico rushed her to the toilet and watched while she dry-heaved a couple of times. She stood and washed her hands and face and rallied. He quickly poured her a glass of water, saying, "Would you like to lie down? I'm sorry if I've upset you."

"No, I'm not upset. I just don't feel very well. Your family is so warm and lovely, how could any of this upset me? I can see how each of your parents complement one another now that I understand the relationship. Who am I to say there is anything wrong with their… union?"

Nico breathed a sigh of relief. He hoped she really meant what she said; she seemed sincere about it.

"Can we *please* go and get something to eat? I don't remember ever being so hungry."

Nico thought the hunger and the nausea together sounded odd, but he answered, "Of course, my dearest. Let's go." As they walked back toward the dining room, he noticed that Eden's hand felt clammy, and she still had an odd pallor, so he stopped her and looked closely into her eyes. "When did you last menstruate?"

That brought a bit of color to her cheeks at least, but then her eyes widened as if in horror. "Oh no. Nico, I must be pregnant! That's why I feel so wretched all of a sudden. I haven't bled since we were together at The Discovery. I've been so occupied, I completely forgot."

A warm excitement buzzed through Nico as he thought about having a blue-eyed son or daughter, and his next thought was, *I can't wait to tell Matty—oh wait… I can't*. Then he wrapped his arms around her saying, "That's wonderful news. You've made me so happy."

"Are you sure?" His embrace was comforting, so she snuggled in to get closer to his chest.

"Of course! I'm excited to tell my family the good news. We'll just want to be married sooner than expected, that's all. Unless you want to wait..."

"Um, no. I see no reason to wait. I would marry you today if you wanted to."

"Then let's go have something to eat and then go find the priest."

"Um… I'm Lutheran… not a very good one though."

Nico laughed softly and answered, "Don't worry, I'm a terrible Catholic. The parish priest here is a family friend though. He'll help us—or we'll find a judge. But Father Andrew has dined at our table many, many times. In fact, I'm surprised he wasn't here to greet us when we arrived. He must have been busy."

Eden wondered briefly whether it was the priest's absence that had made Nico look so disappointed earlier. But… that didn't make a lot of sense to her. Nico had never mentioned Father Andrew before. However, he hadn't been all that forthcoming with information about anyone at home, she now realized. It was too late to back out of marrying him because of the baby, but she fervently hoped there weren't any *more* major surprises—like having three parents. She would have to get used to that idea.

She still had a quizzical look on her face as they sat down

with Nico's parents at the dining room table. Nico was grinning broadly.

Eden couldn't help noticing that the joy his smile projected didn't seem to reach his eyes.

"Where did the rest of the guests go?" he asked as they sat down to a lovely luncheon of fresh, wonderfully seasoned seafood and vegetables.

"They all thoughtfully agreed," Suzette answered, "that we needed to get acquainted with Eden and spend time welcoming you back in a more private setting."

Nico let out a sigh and grinned. "Probably a good idea because we have some more news for you that is somewhat personal."

"The baby?" Suzette asked.

Eden gasped. "How could you know?"

Laughing delightedly, Suzette answered, "My dear one, I have had five children. You develop a sixth sense after a few pregnancies. Our friend Adeline only had to look at me to tell me I was pregnant with Ondine while I was still completely unaware. I thought I was suddenly dying of a terrible malady that made me want to do nothing more than sleep and vomit."

"This is fantastic news! Congratulations," Walter beamed at them.

"We're thrilled for you," Isaac said and raised his glass. "To the next Stark-James, and to his or her lucky parents."

"Thank you all, but I hope my own parents are as thrilled and understanding about this as you are," Eden replied.

Suzette gave a tiny snort and tried to cover it with her napkin. "*We* have no right to call the kettle black," she muttered.

"We'll just marry before we go and tell them," Nico declared. "They can't say much about it then." He looked at his parents and said, "After lunch, I think we'll go find Father Andrew and see about a wedding."

"I'm sure he'll be delighted, Nicolo," Suzette said, beaming at them. "He has asked about you frequently while you were gone, but he does not know about Eden."

That made Eden pause. She had certainly been writing to her family that she was seeing a wonderful young man who was to become a doctor. That they never answered her letters wasn't much of a concern. She knew how busy they were with the ranch. She had not yet had the opportunity to tell them that Nico had proposed, however. Why would Nico not have told his parents about her sooner? Was he less sure of her than he'd let on?

"I did tell you we were coming home together, Maman, and you knew we were planning to marry."

"Yes, but that was only a week ago; I have not seen Father Andrew since then."

Hearing that made Eden feel somewhat better, but she still wondered why he wasn't more informative about her to his family.

Suzette continued, "We should have Marguerite design a wedding gown for you, Eden. She is retired now, but she was a magnificent fashion designer in France and then in San Francisco—sought after by everyone who wanted to look their best. She would be honored to do this for you as Doc Louis has such a special relationship with Nicolo. They feel like extended family anyway."

"Oh, I'm not sure I could afford anything like a custom-designed gown…" Eden tried to protest.

"Don't even think of it. It will be our pleasure to pay Marguerite for her artistry—if she even asks for payment. She might just want to do it for a lark."

Eden thought of how long a special gown might take to make, and she felt as if the sand was quickly running out of her personal hourglass. Nevertheless, she smiled and said, "What an honor. I don't know what to say except thank you very much."

"When you get back from seeing Father Andrew, we'll have Marguerite measure you. You'll be surprised at how quickly she can work," Suzette added. She could see the worry in the young woman's eyes.

"Let's not wear Eden out, Maman. She is terribly tired, you know."

"Yes, Nicolo. I am aware. Marguerite can come here. She is only a short walk up the street, after all. After that, Eden can have a rest."

The Stark-James parents proceeded to ask Eden question after question about her family and their cattle ranch. While she spoke fondly of her parents and brothers, it quickly became obvious to all of them she had no desire to return to that way of life. Walter seemed especially understanding and told her, "Nicolo's godfather Uncle Royal was raised on a dairy farm in New York, and he couldn't wait to leave." He nodded sagely. "The two of you probably have a lot in common."

Throughout the conversation, Eden noted how affectionately all three of Nico's parents spoke to one another. It was nothing like her family. They made eye contact and gave each other sweet smiles as if to say, "Wait until we're alone."

She felt the palpable attraction amongst them; it made her want to yank Nico back down the hall and rip his clothes off. She wondered what had come over her. Before today, she was definitely attracted to Nico and looked forward to sharing his bed again, but the fierceness of this desire was new. She thought she might combust if they weren't given the chance for some alone time… soon.

♡♡♡

ALTHOUGH EDEN WAS MORE THAN READY FOR A NAP WHEN lunch ended, she also wanted fervently to get this wedding accomplished now that she knew she was with child. It couldn't happen fast enough, as far as she was concerned. She had meant it when she said that *today* would be fine with her.

"May we go see your priest now?" she asked Nico as soon as the dishes were cleared away.

"Absolutely. Shall we walk or take a carriage? It's only about fifteen minutes away on foot."

"It's a beautiful day, and I'd love to walk." Eden had no desire to get into another moving vehicle after her train ride. So, off they went with instructions to offer greetings to Father Andrew from Nico's parents.

"Be sure to invite him to dinner soon," Suzette said.

When they arrived at the church, which was a beautiful structure in the Spanish mission style, Nico led Eden around to the side of the building to the office entrance. Entering the room, they encountered a young nun who was dusting Father Andrew's desk. She jumped a couple of inches in the air when the door opened.

"Good afternoon, Sister. Sorry to startle you. We're here to see Father Andrew. Is he available?"

Her eyes dropped to look at the floor as she spoke. "N… no. He's away g… g… giving last rights. B… but F… F… Father De… De… De…" She huffed. "Matthew is in the sanctuary." Her final words tumbled out quickly, and her face turned crimson.

"Oh! He must be new since I went away. Thank you, Sister. We'll just go find him then." As he led Eden out of an interior door to the sanctuary, he said softly, "Let's hope this Father Matthew is as nice a fellow as Father Andrew."

In the otherwise deserted sanctuary, Nico looked around until he saw the silhouette of a tall, broad-shouldered priest standing in front of a stained-glass window as if studying its story. The window depicted Eve being tempted by the serpent, and suddenly Nico smiled and wondered if this was somehow prophetic. Eden. He'd seen that window himself probably hundreds of times and never thought about the significance. Then his mind caught on the thought that Eden was his own personal garden of delight, and he squeezed her hand.

"Excuse me, Father?" Nico spoke loudly across the large space, obviously interrupting the man's reverie. Father Matthew jerked and spun around with a surprised look on his face. Eden gasped inwardly at the man's incandescent beauty; *no one* had the right to be that attractive.

The priest didn't notice her reaction. Instead, he was staring at Nico with an unreadable expression. There was recognition there, Eden was sure of that, but something else, too—something far deeper. Sadness and happiness and confusion and… could it be passion?… all wrapped up in a stormy gaze.

The priest's eyes drifted down from Nico's face to his body, and then to his hand, currently clasped in her own. Concerned that the show of affection might be improper in a house of worship, she pulled away.

Nico didn't notice. He made a strangled sound and rushed toward the priest—leaving her alone.

Both men ran the final few steps toward one another and crashed together, wrapping their arms tightly around one another, and oddly, they both seemed to be crying and laughing at the same time. This had to be the strangest thing she'd ever seen. Nico had embraced her plenty of times with affection, but this display spoke of desperation, elation, and sorrow. As they finally separated a little, they looked into each other's eyes and were suddenly *kissing*. Passionately.

Eden let out an anguished cry and thought she might faint. She dropped into the closest pew and put her hands over her face. But then she had to look again as if she were a moth drawn to a flame. As much as she wanted to look away, she could not. Despite the tears pouring down her face, the sight stirred something profound within her, and she had no name for it.

Father Matthew was the first to pull back, saying, "Sorry. *Sorry.* This is wrong, Nico. We can't. I can't."

Nico remembered himself suddenly and spun around looking for Eden. He rushed to her and took her hand, trying to encourage her into a standing position. It wasn't working. She snatched her hand away as if his touch caused her pain.

"Just let me be, Nico," she sobbed. "I need to gather myself." Eden shook all over.

"I need to explain."

"No one is stopping you, though I'm not sure it needs much explanation," she said between hiccupping gulps and moans. She wrapped her arms around her stomach and rocked forward and back in the pew. "Obviously, you love someone else, and you've used me! I've been a complete fool." She wouldn't look at him, but she stole a glance at Father Matthew, who had followed Nico toward her.

She couldn't quite get over the priest's beauty. She had thought Nico was the most attractive man she'd ever known, but this person looked like an angel, he was so perfect. But… a priest? She was ready to go to confession for her thoughts right then and there, and she wasn't even a Catholic. *How can I even contemplate such a thing? Nico has betrayed me in the worst possible way, and I'm looking at this man with longing? I've lost my mind.*

Nico gave up trying to get Eden to stand up, so he sat down next to her, wrapped an arm around her to quell her shakes and make her stop rocking. He looked up and asked, "So, you're *Father* Matthew now? I guess 'Father Matty' would sound rather juvenile, now that I think about it, and you're all grown up, aren't you?"

Matty had added a good six inches of height to his frame since he'd last been in Los Angeles and was now as tall as Nico. Apparently, he'd been a late bloomer.

"It's Father Deacon Matthew Remington actually, but that's rather a mouthful for some people. I haven't taken my final vows yet. I've only been ordained as a deacon so far."

"Ah. Well, let me introduce my fiancée, Eden Godwin. We came to talk to Father Andrew about marrying us." Nico had an edge to his voice that was not all that friendly. He dashed a tear away from his eye, which puzzled Eden as much as their earlier reaction to one another.

Kissing? Anger? Tears? What is going on? She squirmed out of his embrace.

Father Matthew stuck out a hand toward Eden, saying, "Pleased to meet you, Miss Godwin. When are you planning to marry?"

Eden was still for a moment and then reluctantly raised her hand—nearly jolting at the feel of him as his hand closed around hers. She decided she must be reacting to her pregnancy because there was clearly something wrong with her. She suddenly had a fervent desire to kiss this man the same way Nico had done. She locked eyes with him, and a bolt of something like recognition sizzled between them. They'd never laid eyes on one another, but it was as if they'd known each other for years. Eden's shock was mirrored in Father Matthew's eyes.

And such magnificent eyes they were. Bright and dazzling like a summer sky.

Staring unabashedly at him, she noticed he did have a slight imperfection in the shape of his nose, but the small crook in it merely enhanced his appeal. She fervently wanted to hate him but found that impossible.

Father Matthew seemed to shake himself out of a trance and looked back at Nico when no one answered his question. "Nico? The wedding plans?"

"Where's Father Andrew?" Nico asked instead of answering.

"He's out administering the last rights to my father. I was summoned because the old man is dying, and I was needed to settle his estate—among other things. I find, in a most un-

Christian manner, I can barely manage to face him—much to Father Andrew's dismay. I was getting ready to return in a few months anyway to assist at this church, but I was ordered to return post-haste. So, here I am at long last."

"Where have you been?"

"Well, obviously, at school and then seminary." His arms widened to indicate his clothing.

Nico was vibrating with emotion, and Eden could feel it pouring off of him as he suddenly shouted. "And I suppose they don't allow any communication to leave the seminary walls? Matty, I waited and waited to hear from you!" Then he bellowed, "How could you just leave like that and ignore me?" His voice hitched when he asked, "Did I mean *nothing* to you?"

Eden tried to pat Nico's arm to quiet him, and her need to make him feel better confused her even more as Father Matthew said coolly, "Please remember where you are and show some respect. It's obvious we need to talk, but the sanctuary is not the place for such a conversation."

Eden narrowed her eyes at Father Matthew before patting Nico's arm again. This situation was so strange. She could not understand her need to comfort the man who was breaking her heart. This was the most confusing day she'd ever had.

Overwhelmed with emotion, tears cascaded down Eden's face. She cried for Nico's obvious anguish, and she cried for her own grief at being taken for a fool. She cried for her baby's fate, for how could she leave its father, or how could she marry its father knowing he loved another more than he loved her?

Still shouting, Nico jumped to his feet and roared, "Would you prefer to hear it in the confessional, *Father*? Do you want to hear me admit how I'm still desperately and futilely in love with a man who is now a *priest*, and I am also engaged to this wonderful, enchanting woman who is having my baby, and I impregnated her without marrying her first because I was so desperate to prove to her my love that I couldn't wait? And now she probably hates me—with good reason—because I was too cowardly to tell her anything about my family or about you because I was scared she wouldn't love me back if she knew. Won't that be a great pile of sins to absolve? Oh, and let's not forget the burning *hatred* I harbor for your wretched, dying father. Quick, tell me to pray on it! I'm a rotten sinner who is not worthy of anyone's love—least of all my precious Eden's. And… I haven't even been able to stomach going to mass since the day you disappeared."

Returning his ire with an equally loud volume, Matty yelled back, "I'm not a priest yet! I cannot absolve your sins because I can't administer holy sacraments—not even last rites! I can marry and bury people, but I cannot grant absolution. I'm still just a deacon—and apparently not a very righteous one—considering the way I feel about you." His chest heaved and he clenched and unclenched his fists. In a softer voice, he pled with Nico, "Please, let's go to my house where we can have some privacy. We're probably scandalizing Sister

Mary Gertrude. She's so timid, the poor woman can't even speak properly in front of me."

"It's not just you. We encountered that as well," Nico muttered.

"Huh. She speaks just fine around Father Andrew and everyone else."

As her gaze bounced back and forth between them, Eden thought she had a good idea why these two men had such an effect on the nun. They apparently robbed the woman of her senses. Even in their rage and sorrow, they both exuded a raw, sexual energy.

"Isn't your disgusting father at your house?" Nico snapped. "I'm surprised you'd want to be anywhere near that man."

"He's at the clinic waiting to die. When Doc Louis called the seminary, they ordered me home to say my final goodbye and forgive him to his face," Matty snorted bitterly.

"So everyone knew where you were but me? Has everyone I know been lying to me?"

"Quit feeling so sorry for yourself. You're not the only heartbroken person here." His eyes flicked to Eden briefly, and Eden thought she saw a flash of regret. "But no. No one knew until recently. The situation with my father escalated when his liver began to fail, and Father Andrew told Doc Louis about my whereabouts. He figured my father was beyond being able to do anything to me at that point. But, Nico, please, let's all go to my house. I'm terribly uncomfortable here in the sanctuary talking about my father… and… us."

"Don't you have servants? They'll hear us too, you know. And they can be big gossips if that's what you're worried about."

"They're all gone. I'll have to at least hire a cook, but I haven't had the time yet, nor do I have any money to pay for one until the estate is settled. I've only been back for a couple of days, and all I've done so far is see my father briefly and try to clean up the place." He gave Nico a flat look. "You can imagine."

"Yes, I guess I can."

"I'll just tell Sister Mary Gertrude where I'm going and that I'll be gone for the rest of the day. Father Andrew will be back soon, and he'll understand. He knows I needed to see you when you arrived. I just didn't know it would be so soon… and with such lovely company." He tried to smile at Eden, but instead looked melancholy and confused.

"I certainly didn't expect to see you, but no one told you we were arriving today?"

"No." Matty left them for a moment to speak to the nun, and during that respite, Eden still refused to look at Nico as he sat down beside her again. He could hardly blame her. It had to be difficult to hear that the man she loved also loved someone else—to witness the two of them kissing. Nico's heart ached for the pain he had caused. He knew he should give her space, but when Eden tried to scoot away from him, he held fast to her. He couldn't let her go.

Despite his arm around her shoulder, Eden had now concluded that Nico obviously loved Father Matthew with deeper fervor than he'd ever felt for her, and he'd loved him for far longer. He probably just needed her to work in his clinic after all, and that's why he wanted to marry her—to make sure she'd come home with him. If she didn't have a baby to consider, she might just go back to Capistrano and marry some boring cattleman. But that wouldn't be right. Not for the cattleman or for her.

And someone had to do the right thing—no matter how badly it hurt. She had very few choices, but the most logical one might also be the most difficult. A deep river of regret stretched out in front of Eden, rippling grief and sadness that she imagined would stay with her for the rest of her life.

She'd never imagined pain like this. It was one thing to be disappointed by someone you didn't care about, but to be betrayed by the love of your life was inconceivable.

When Nico nuzzled her neck and said softly, "I'm so sorry, Eden. I truly love you so deeply," her heart cracked. She didn't believe him—couldn't believe him. Not after what she had just seen. She was certain that was a platitude to make her less emotional.

It wasn't going to work.

CHAPTER
Ten

Eden finally turned to Nico, who looked positively haunted, and said stiffly, "It appears there are several things you've been keeping from me. I can't help but wonder how many more revelations there will be. And I wonder if I'm in love with someone who is merely a figment of my imagination." She extricated herself from his hold and walked rigidly toward the sanctuary door where she waited for the two men. She was bone weary and wanted desperately to rest and be alone with her worries. Removing a lace-edged handkerchief from her reticule, she attempted to dry her eyes and compose herself as she faced the heavy, closed door.

Matty returned quickly and led them out of the church and toward his home. Eden halted, however, saying, "I'll just head back to your house, Nico. This discussion is for the two of you."

She turned resolutely… and then realized she didn't know where she was or how to get back.

Gently taking her arm, Nico said, "You don't even know the way, Eden, and it's not safe for you to wander around alone in a strange city. We came into the church building on another side, so I'm sure this looks unfamiliar. But mostly, why would you think anything we have to say does not concern you? This is all about you as much as Matty and me."

"I'm not sure about that," Eden said in a shaky voice. "The two of you have history that obviously has nothing to do with me."

"We have history, yes, but we need to discuss our future, and you are very much an important part of that. Please relax and come with us. It's not far to Matty's place. It's only halfway between here and my family's house."

Conceding to herself that she was turned around and would no doubt become terribly lost if she ventured out on her own, Eden agreed.

No one spoke until they were inside Matty's house, and he escorted them to the main salon. Nico tried to encourage Eden toward a comfortable settee but was dismayed that she chose to sit across the room from him in a chair by herself. Her face was a stoic mask, and she had her handkerchief clutched in her hand.

Matty had avoided his father's study so far, not wanting to revisit the memory of the last time he was in that room. He wondered if there were still nasty stains on the floor from his retaliation for the busted lip his father had given him. That seemed preposterous after so many years, but the possibility bothered him. As much as he despised the kind of person his father had become, the guilt of smashing the man's head with a heavy wooden box still haunted him. Matty sometimes felt the weight of his sin dragging him down, and he thought perhaps he didn't deserve any happiness. Confession had not unburdened his mind as it should have.

This room was in pretty good shape, however. All it had needed was some dusting and airing out because his father had never used the room for much. It had been his mother's domain when she'd entertained visitors.

Most of the house had fallen into disrepair in his time away. Since returning, Matty had concentrated his heaviest efforts on the wrecked kitchen and his former bedroom, which had become a receptacle for old bottles and assorted refuse. It was as if his father had wanted to throw his trash at Matty in absentia.

Standing in front of the cold fireplace, Matty began, "First of all, Nico, I know I owe you a tremendous apology for not getting in touch, but I swear to you, I tried repeatedly." He noted Nico's skeptical expression and continued, "I was sent to a strict religious school run by monks. Father Andrew stressed that I would be safe there because it was remote and not well known, though it had a good reputation for academics. I believe that most, if not all, of the boys who were there had experienced some kind of trouble. I never tried to find out more because I was reluctant to share my own story. The brothers had rules for everything, and one of them was that students were to have no communication outside of the school with anyone except for a monthly letter home to parents for the students who had them." He gave a resigned look. "Well, I certainly wasn't going to write to my father and let him know of my whereabouts, and he obviously wouldn't have passed along any letters to you if he'd received them. So I tried to send letters to your parents, telling the monks they were my guardians. That just bought me a mountain of punishment for telling lies, so I finally gave up. Apparently, Father Andrew had been very clear about my parentage and that he was the only one who knew of my location for every-one's safety.

"I did hear from Father Andrew from time to time, so I knew only that you and your family were well, but he just communicated through the brothers—not to me directly. He didn't want any mail addressed to me that might be intercepted by someone my father paid off at the post office. When I left that school and headed to seminary, I heard you had left Los Angeles and were in medical school—though I had no idea where—and that my father's condition was deteriorating." He hung his head. "I'm sorry to say, I was not saddened by this bit of news about him. Apparently, the monks did *not* manage to instill a good Christian attitude of forgiveness in me. In fair-ness, it wasn't their area of interest. They preferred to spend their time teaching me to be a rule follower and religious scholar." He sighed. "At least some of the brothers were excellent teachers, so there was one bright light about my exile."

"Excuse me, Father Matthew…" Eden interrupted from her chair across the room.

"No, please, I'm Matty to you and Nico."

"Yes, well, Matty then. May I know why it was so vital to keep you away from your father? I can tell there is no love lost for the man from either of you, so I'm curious as to why that is."

Nico spoke up when Matty looked sick. "His father is a despicable drunkard who used Matty's body as a punching bag and nearly killed him. Matty showed up at our house bloodied and bruised more times than I can count. Then finally, when we were sixteen, his father broke Matty's nose and ribs, and my family and friends conspired to keep the man away from him so he could heal."

With wide eyes, she asked, "Why did he treat Matty so horribly?"

Matty spoke up finally, "He never needed a plausible reason. I was young and smaller than him, and I was available to bully and ridicule with cutting, horrible words. He was a miserable drunk with nothing better to do. When he wasn't drunk, he largely ignored me, but after he got into the whiskey, he would blame me for everything. Sometimes he would think I looked too much like my mother, so he'd smack me in the face. He would get the notion that I was a horrible son who caused her to get sick and die, so he'd punch me. Or maybe he was upset over losing a game of cards, and he would go into a tirade about my uselessness. Anything would set him off, and I was his scapegoat. Early on, I hoped I could reason with him, but when I tried, it usually just escalated the problem. It was when he brutally attacked a trusted friend and started swinging a gun around that his actions got the attention of the police. That was when I had to leave so no one would get killed."

"Did you ever fight back?" she asked, horrified.

"Twice." He nodded and sighed. "The first time I slapped him to keep him away, so he slugged me in the face and broke my nose, I stumbled and fell, and he fractured my ribs by repeatedly applying his *boot* to my body as hard as he could. The second time I fought back was when he dragged me home from Nico's house where I'd been staying to recover from my broken ribs. I was mightily relieved when Nico's fathers showed up with the police. That was the last time I saw him until yesterday. I know I was supposed to be there to forgive him, but I could barely look at him. So much for turning the other cheek. I'm afraid the years apart did nothing to make me forget his cruelty. I used to hope I could help him, but I gradually began to realize I was young and idealistic. I was a fool. He was not going to be a loving father anymore—never the way he was when my mother was alive."

"I see. I'm terribly sorry to hear this, Matty, but I'm sure you were an optimistically trusting son—not a fool."

Matty's tense jaw loosened by just a fraction at Eden's words. "Well, thank you for your confidence in me, even though it's probably misplaced. I'm not that good of a person, you see." With a resolute expression, Matty explained, "Father Andrew knew I had a deep interest in religious history and philosophy and took that to mean I was destined to become a priest. He stepped in and orchestrated my future, assuming he was doing the right thing for everyone by sending me away to school. He made a deal with the diocese that they would pay for my tuition and living expenses if I would eventually return and serve here as a parish priest." Matty looked down at his hands. "Father Andrew is a good man and a wonderful priest, but I wish sometimes that he'd asked me then what it was I wanted for my own future. Now I'm trapped by the commitment he forced me into."

Nico gasped. "Have you discussed this with him recently?"

"I've tried to, but he reminds me of my duty to God and to the diocese."

"Seems a bit much, dragging God into it," Eden said with a frown.

"Well, perhaps, but consider the source. He is a man of God. Also, I'm beginning to suspect that he has aspirations of becoming a bishop, and if he has me as his protégé, it makes him appear successful and important. He's a lot more ambitious than I ever realized, and I feel like I'm a pawn in his chess game," Matty answered. Looking at Nico, he asked, "Will you *please* accept my most heartfelt apology, Nico? It was killing me—as I assumed it was you—that I couldn't get in touch. I could hardly announce to the brothers that I was deeply in love with you and knew I'd broken your heart and needed to make you understand why. Even if I had managed to explain, they probably would have thought we were just children who would grow out of our feelings." A hot tear cascaded down his cheek, and he scraped it away roughly with the back of his hand.

Eden flinched as Matty expressed his love for Nico and had to dab her eyes a few more times. *Matty's story breaks my heart! But how can Nico possibly love me if he's loved Matty for so long? Even if he were to choose me, I would always wonder if I was his second choice.*

Nico looked stiff as he spoke. "Maybe you should have tried, Matty. Priests are human, after all. But what I want to know is, why did you continue on with seminary unless you were prepared to become a priest?" He was not quite ready to give up his anger and accept an apology. "And I wonder how many times Father Andrew had to confess to lying. He told me he had no knowledge of your whereabouts."

"Maybe he was evading the truth for what he felt was a good reason, or he split hairs because he didn't know my exact location on that particular day. I don't know," Matty sighed. "He was probably afraid he would hear that you'd run away from home looking for me and shirking your responsibility to Doc Louis. He is all about responsibility, after all." Nico looked like he was considering that response, so Matty continued, "To answer your other question, I guess I continued on with seminary because it was what was expected of me, and I needed *someone's* approval after never getting any from my father. I didn't want to let people down who'd invested in my future. Everyone I cared about seemed lost to me, and I felt awfully isolated… even abandoned. I know that was no one's fault, but I was so lonely. At least this way I had a goal —even if it wasn't the one I chose. It was easiest to just keep going."

"Matty, it's *your* life! Your future. Not the community's or the church's or Father Andrew's. Have you ever considered what it is *you* want to do?"

"Yes, I have. I've always wanted to teach. I love the church, and I love Catholicism, but I love it as a historical and philosophical framework from which to work—not as a vocation in and of itself. You know I've always liked discussing and debating what I've read." He hung his head briefly and looked up. "I don't feel as though I have some special link to the Almighty or even that I need to serve God, even though I love God." He put his face into his hands for a moment. "I feel so conflicted. I've taken preliminary vows as a deacon, and they expect me to take my final vows soon to become ordained as a priest, but I'm afraid I have too much sin in my heart to take the job seriously. And yet I'm afraid to let Father Andrew down at this point."

"But aren't you working hard to be a good person?" Eden asked. "You seem quite careful about how to lead your life, judging by what little I know of you and from my own observations." She glared at Nico. "Nico had, unfortunately, neglected to enlighten me of your existence until today."

Capturing her attention back to him, Matty explained, "Whether I seem like a good person or not, I am a sinner. Right at this very moment, I have contempt in my heart that I should have purged a long time ago. I have done things for which I've never properly atoned. I am teetering on the precipice of dishonoring someone who has mentored me and looked out for me." His eyes blazed. "Because what I most want to do is drag Nico upstairs and make unholy love to him for hours… and make him mine forever." He paused for a second and let that sink in and then continued in a softer tone, "And… since I'm being honest… I'd love to do the same thing to you. I also ironically find that I have this incredible and undeniable urge to impregnate you, and I think it's a shame that deed is already done."

Eden drew in a sharp breath, and Nico shuddered at her side, but neither interrupted Matty, who choked out a mirthless, sarcastic groan. "You can obviously add jealousy to my faults. I can't have Nico because he's promised to you, while I am contracted to the demands of the diocese. And now Nico presents me with an additional temptation in the form of the loveliest woman I've ever seen. This is pure cruelty."

Eden's chin dropped at the same time Nico let out a loud laugh, and then he said, "Well! My unorthodox family has made a rather big impression on you. Good for them!" Then he looked at Eden and said, "Depending on how you feel, what Matty is implying could be the solution to some of our problems."

Eden's eyes widened, but she couldn't form the words to speak just yet.

"Whoa, whoa, Nico. I'm not suggesting we have an arrangement like your family," Matty said. "If we did that, we would just be in a bigger mess."

Nico frowned. "I don't see why. At least we'd be happy—that is, if Eden agrees to it. Become a priest, don't become a priest—that's up to you. You'll be sinning in someone's eyes no matter what you do."

CHAPTER
Eleven

MATTY SUDDENLY REMEMBERED WHERE HE'D BEEN STANDING and the thoughts that had been flitting through his mind in the moments before Nico called out to him in the sanctuary. "Are you trying to be like the snake, Nico?" he asked softly, his brow wrinkled in confusion and pain. "Are you really trying to tempt me into even more sin?"

"I'm merely suggesting one possible solution that would be mutually pleasurable. You know you'd love it, Matty." Turning to Eden, he asked, "And what about you? You were very accepting when it became clear that I was raised with two fathers who love each other as deeply as they love my mother. You said yourself that they complement each other, and you saw nothing wrong with their union. I hope you were speaking from your heart and not trying to placate me."

"That's true," Eden answered shakily. "I am not the least bit put off by your family. However, this is a highly unusual situation you're asking me to consider, and nothing I've ever seen for myself. Besides, I don't even know Matty."

Nico's eyes sparkled, and his expression turned mischievous. "Why don't you kiss him and get a better idea of what he's like then?"

"Nico!"

"I'm serious. At least come closer to me. I don't like seeing you so far away by yourself." He stood and strode to her, encouraging her gently out of her chair and over to the settee he'd vacated. When she was seated, he turned to Matty and did the same thing, escorting him to sit beside Eden. When they both looked at him wide-eyed and as stiff as boards, he knelt on the carpet between them. He leaned in and wrapped his arms around Eden, whispered how deeply he loved her and began kissing her so passionately it made her toes curl. When he felt her relax, he pulled back and grasped one of her hands. With the other hand, he reached for Matty's neck and pulled him forward as Matty let out a moan that went from tortured to accepting in a flash. The two men began kissing with equal fervor.

Seeing these two men engaging this way up close made Eden feel as though she might melt right off the furniture into a puddle on the floor. It was one thing to see them embrace the first time, when she was overcome with shock and dismay and standing at a distance. But now, watching from mere inches away, she could hear the soft, satisfied noises they made and feel the energy pulsating through them. She could hardly catch her breath—they were just so… *beautiful* was the only word that came to mind. Her heart sped up as she realized she wanted to be part of that spectacle more than anything.

What is wrong with me? I should be furious with Nico. She tried to hang onto that anger, but it dissolved as both men pulled apart and leaned into her simultaneously and as smoothly as a well-oiled machine might. Nico whispered, "Go ahead. Do it," as he nibbled and kissed her neck beneath her ear in precisely the way he knew she loved. After only a momentary pause, Matty groaned with his surrender and claimed her mouth. He was powerless to fight his need.

Matty's kiss was rougher than Nico's. His felt more desperate, more demanding somehow, although Eden had very little experience to go on since Nico's kisses were her only frame of reference. When she kissed Nico, it was always delightful. He was never demanding, and he was patient almost to the point of frustration. But she loved his sweetness and knew deep within her that she truly adored him.

Matty had no patience. No control. He consumed her; kissing him felt like being swept up in a swirling tropical storm. In the back of her mind, she considered how they harmonized with one another. Somehow, being with both of them made Eden feel more complete herself.

Matty's storm began building and building within her. She became aware she'd been so caught off-guard in the shock and devastation of his kisses she hadn't realized Nico had slid his hand beneath her skirt and between her legs. He was stroking her rhythmically and speaking sweet words of love and encouragement into her ear. As Matty's tongue plundered her mouth, Nico's fingers drew a relentless pattern on her most sensitive area. He increased the speed and pressure until she cried out in a release that was so enormous, she feared she might faint. Nico chuckled, and Matty sat back and watched as Nico removed his hand from under her dress.

"I've never kissed a woman before now," Matty stated thoughtfully and then added with a grin, "I liked it."

Eden's voice shook as she put her trembling fingers to her mouth. "I've never kissed anyone but Nico."

"Then we find that we have something in common," Matty laughed.

"*I've* never enjoyed kissing as much as this," Nico added. "Individually, you're both delights, but together, you're magnificent."

Eden could now understand this way of thinking.

"You really are the snake," Matty said wistfully and then sighed. "Now that this has happened, I'm just going to feel more torn up inside."

"Oh dear," Eden said softly. "Matty, do you have a telephone here?"

Wondering who on earth needed to hear about their activities, he blinked at her. "No. Why?"

She looked at Nico. "Your mother was expecting us back at your house so I could talk to her friend Marguerite about making me a dress. It would be rude not to arrive on time."

"So you still want to marry me? I haven't put you off, have I?"

"Nico…" Eden sighed, "It's not about what I want. I *have* to marry you. We're having a baby. I just don't know about… anything else." She looked pointedly at Matty who looked equal parts sad, baffled, and ready for more. *I suppose I still need… want to marry Nico—for the sake of the baby if nothing else, but Matty will certainly become an issue between us… or he could be something wonderful with us.* Eden knew she had a lot to talk about with Nico, but her mind was reeling with all that had come to light in the past few hours—Nico's family and upbringing, her pregnancy, *Matty*. It was a lot for one mind to consider, and her magnificent climax had scrambled her brains.

"I sincerely hope that isn't the only reason you still want to marry me, but we can talk about it some more later. If Marguerite and Maman are waiting, we'd better head home then. Come with us back to the house, Matty. My parents will be thrilled to see you, and they'll expect you to stay for dinner."

Matty grinned sheepishly, "I probably won't manage to eat much unless I join you. Cooking is not one of my skills.

Thank you, Nico. I'd love to see them too." He added in a serious tone of voice, "What just happened was… uplifting and enjoyable, but it doesn't solve a thing."

"We'll see," Nico said, sounding happier than Eden had ever heard him. "It might just solve everything after all. And you wouldn't want to kiss the lady and then desert her, now, would you? It's considered very bad form, you know."

Matty shook his head with a wry look. "You're trouble." But he took Eden's hand and squeezed it, then placed a sweet kiss on her lips that was nothing like the lightning bolts he'd kissed her with before. He was conflicted.

Nico shrugged, "I'm practical. Listen, Matty, do you want to go put on some clothes that are a little less… *priestly*?"

Matty cocked his head and admitted, "This is all I've been wearing for the past couple of years, and I don't exactly fit any of my old clothes. You may have noticed I've grown a bit since I left. It would make me ill to go look for something of my father's to put on. Anyway, this collar has been mandatory since 1884. I'm stuck with these clothes unless I formally resign."

"So you would consider a lay position or a teaching job?" Nico asked hopefully.

"I'm considering everything. But my clothes are the least of my worries. Shall we go?"

♡♡♡

SUZETTE AND MARGUERITE HAD THEIR HEADS TOGETHER looking at swatches of material when Nico barged in announcing, "Maman! Look at who Eden and I found! *Father Matthew* will be staying to dinner if that suits you."

Suzette gasped and sprang from her seat. She rushed to Matty, throwing her arms around him and kissing both cheeks the same way she'd greeted Nico. "Matty! We have all missed you terribly. Let me look at you. You are so tall now, and so grown up! Still as handsome as ever. You are a priest? Does this make you happy? You will stay for dinner of course!"

Suzette's embrace brought tears to Matty's eyes. "I've missed all of you so badly, I thought some days I couldn't survive, Miss Suzette. Thank you, I'd love to stay for dinner." *Or maybe forever.*

She made a small clucking noise almost like a mother hen as she patted his back. "How is your father?"

"Dying. Father Andrew left to give him last rights earlier today, but I didn't… couldn't go with him." Matty's head dropped. "I think Father Andrew would have argued with me about it more if he hadn't been told to hurry."

"I think even God would understand that you do not need to feel any remorse about that, my sweet boy."

Nico laughed softly and pointed out, "Matty is hardly a boy, Maman."

"Ah, mais non. You, Warren, Bay, *and* Matty will always be my boys!" She hugged Matty one more time before letting him go.

Eden could see that Suzette was being honest by the fierce look in her eyes. *How marvelous to be loved so unconditionally by this splendid woman. I don't believe I've ever seen such emotion from my parents, and yet I've never doubted their love. Now I wonder, though—do they love me like this?*

"Nicolo, please go ask Cook to bring Eden some refreshment and tell her we will have one more for dinner. Your fiancée is looking pale again. She will need a variety of flavors to nibble on. Cook will understand if you tell her she is enceinte." Turning to Eden, she ordered, "Please have a seat, and Marguerite and I will show you what we have been discussing. But if nothing suits you, do not be afraid to speak up and put us firmly in our place." Looking at her son, she added, "After you speak to Cook, go perhaps to sit in the library until the men get back and we can have our dinner? You will not be interested in dresses." She added with a wink at Eden, "Or woman talk."

"Oh, yes, right. I'll take care of that now, Maman." Then he grinned and said to her in French, *"Now that Matty has returned, the three of us have a chance for wonderful possibilities, don't you agree?"* Suzette and Marguerite smiled happily at him. Eden wondered what he'd said.

Nico would have led Matty to his room, but it occurred to him that perhaps those surroundings might be too much to take for the both of them. So much had been said and done in that room, and as much as Nico wanted Matty to be a part of his life again in the same way as before, he did understand that

Matty was having a crisis with his conscience. Nico wouldn't stop pushing and cajoling, however.

On their way to the kitchen, it occurred to him that Matty never answered his mother's question about whether he was happy and had not clarified anything about being a priest either. He stored that away as something positive to analyze later.

♡♡♡

ONCE THEY WERE ALONE, SUZETTE REGARDED EDEN contemplatively. Eden began to blush and didn't even know why until Suzette opened her mouth finally and uttered words Eden never expected.

"If you were to choose to be with both of them at the same time, your life could be full of delights you've never imagined."

Eden gasped and asked, "Has Nico said something to you?"

The older women smiled knowingly at each other, then Suzette answered, "Not in so many words, my dear one, but you just confirmed my suspicions, and I know my son. I do not doubt his love for you, and I know he has loved Matty his entire life—not just as a best friend but as a lover and a forever mate. I also saw how Matty looks at you and Nicolo, and I see both desire and confusion in your eyes."

Marguerite studied Eden's expression as well and added,

"If you have any questions at all, we are the women to ask. We, as well as Adeline, have plenty of experience."

Blushing even more deeply, Eden blurted out, "You and Doc Louis have a third? Oh! Pardon me. That's an impertinent question and none of my business."

With a wistful expression, Marguerite answered, "No. I was referring to the life I had with my late husband in France before I left and came to California. With Louis, we never found ourselves attached to anyone enough to bring him into the fold. Well… there was one gentleman we considered, but he ever so politely turned us down before we had the chance." She smiled slyly at Suzette who returned her secretive look.

"Thank you both, but things are more complicated for us. With the baby coming, Nico and I need to marry as soon as possible, and Matty has vows to take. He is supposed to be living a life of celibacy anyway, as I understand. I'm not a Catholic; I was raised Lutheran…"

Suzette interrupted, "So you are saying that Matty is not a priest yet? Why is he dressing like one?"

"That's right. He's a deacon, but soon…"

"Forget *soon*!' Suzette gestured forcefully. "He is not a priest then, and he has not made that big mistake yet. Matty needs a family more than any young man I have ever known. You need to make him see that, Eden."

"I can't… You… don't think he should become a priest?"

"Absolutely not. He loves God, and he is religious, but he does not belong celibate the rest of his life. That would be a sin against all that is holy. And I say this as a Catholic. I know that young man—almost as well as my own son Nicolo. Matty will hate himself for a while no matter what he chooses because he has a bit of a martyr personality. But he needs to make the right choice. Being a priest is the wrong one. When we saw to it that he was sent away to school for his safety, we never had this in mind for his future. He is a scholar with a brilliant, inquisitive mind." Suzette said something in French that sounded suspiciously like a curse to Eden. "How did this happen?"

"From what he says, Father Andrew made the plans and arranged to have the diocese pay for his education and living expenses. Now he has a commitment to them to come back here and serve the community as a priest."

"We shall see about that!" Suzette huffed. "We would have been happy to support the boy, and Father Andrew knew that! Now, we should look at Marguerite's designs and she can show you some fabric. Ah! Here is Cook now. Help yourself, Eden. Have something to nibble on so you can keep up your strength and not feel poorly. If we can do this quickly, perhaps you can lie down and rest for a while before dinner."

"Thank you," Eden said as the cook placed a tray next to her and poured them all cups of tea. "Before we look at any of your lovely plans, I would like to ask you a few things—if you don't mind."

Suzette smiled kindly. "Absolutely. Ask whatever is on your mind."

After waiting for the cook to leave, though she suspected the woman knew everything that went on in this house, Eden asked, "I'm not at all sure this is what I want to begin with, but what could I possibly tell my parents if we were to accept Nico's suggestion and become… three together? It's going to be difficult enough if they realize I'm pregnant."

"Do they ever travel? Would you expect them to come here for a visit?"

Eden almost laughed. "I've never seen them leave the ranch to go anywhere that didn't involve buying or selling cattle. Certainly not for a social visit."

"Then I would expect you would have ample warning should they change their mind and come to Los Angeles."

"Are you suggesting that I lie to them?"

"'Lie' is a strong word. I suggest only that you omit some of the facts unless you think they could accept an unorthodox union for their daughter. My parents lived far from me, and I never felt compelled to write to them and tell them anything other than I was married and happy, and later I wrote to them sporadically to tell them they had more grandchildren. Since I was a mere daughter, they eventually lost interest and concentrated on my eldest brother and his family who remained in France and took over the chateau and managed the estate."

Suzette took a sip of tea. "You could always discuss it with your mother and father in broad terms and see what they have to say before you tell them directly." Indicating the tray of food, she said, "Please eat something. And I am proud of you for even considering this. You will never get any criticism from anyone in this household. None of our other children have chosen such a lifestyle, but they are quite accepting of it, as are their spouses. I knew none of them had it in them to try this until Nicolo came along. He has always been different—more passionate—which is the great irony since he is the non-musical one. He thinks he is different because he does not play an instrument, but he is still very much like his parents. He has his father's appreciation for details, infinite curiosity, and tremendous passion."

"Are you saying you know who his father is?"

"I am saying that Nicolo looks more like me than any of the rest of the children, and in many ways, he embraces the zest and enthusiasm for the world around him that Walter embodies. That is not to say Isaac means any less to him or has not influenced him—because he adores both of his fathers and respects them immensely. It is just a feeling I have always had. I could be wrong, and it could be that he simply enjoys and emulates the way Walter thinks. It does not matter. Nicolo is his own person, and he has his own goals and desires. He will make an excellent husband and father, but he needs Matty in his life. You must be aware of that. Your graceful accep-tance of it—or enthusiastic participation—will make for a far happier marriage for you than if you try to turn a blind eye and make Nicolo do something that will give him terrible guilt."

"I see." Eden looked down pensively and paused. "I have

to marry Nico no matter what, but whether I can trust him is another matter."

Suzette smiled thoughtfully and said, "I understand your concerns, Eden. Nico probably feels awful for not making things clear to you about our family and about his connection to Matty. But in his defense, he did not know if he would ever see Matty again. He may have thought that silence would provide a path to healing. If you could find it in your heart to forgive him, do you think you could accept Matty as well?"

Eden looked at Suzette's earnest expression and answered, "I would never, ever have considered that I would accept such a thing in my life. But having seen you and your husbands, I know there is great love between you all. I love Nico fiercely, and I don't want to put him into a situation that would make him feel guilty, but if we are to proceed, I need to get past the anger I feel right now, knowing I have been kept in the dark about several important aspects of Nico's life." She paused for a moment and then added, "Still, I will consider it—now that I understand it's more than him wanting to have a little fun."

Suzette nodded. "I appreciate that you are open-minded about our chosen lifestyle. You seem like a strong young woman. Nico has chosen well."

"Thank you for saying that, but quite honestly, I have some serious doubts that Nico and I need to address before I can feel right again, and *if* I can, we will have to get Matty to accept both of us. He's an even larger stumbling block; he thinks his commitment to Father Andrew is all-important."

"Yes, well. Nico might have something to say about that. And you as well, when you are ready."

"Maybe so," Eden said, chewing her lower lip thoughtfully.

"You will never regret the decision to accept a third, my dear," Marguerite interjected. "The possibilities for pleasure are incredible." She winked and added, "Now, let me show you some designs."

CHAPTER
Twelve

IN THE LIBRARY, NICO AND MATTY SAT CONTEMPLATING ONE another, Matty drumming his fingers on the arm of his chair nervously. Finally, Nico broke the silence. "You know you want to lead a more normal life. I know you love God, but you aren't a priest."

Matty frowned and snorted, saying, "You call having a wife *and* a husband a normal life?"

Nico shrugged. "It has always been normal around here. Maybe it's not all that ordinary, but why can't we go our own way and make all of us happy?"

"You mean make *you* happy."

"Matty! I resent that. I know it's what you want. You even said so. That talk about wanting to put your own baby in Eden! And she's considering it. I can tell. She's nervous, of course, but you will find that she is a most accepting and adventurous lover. She was a virgin when we met, but she embraces her sexual desires and was never once timid with me. She's amazing. I love her so deeply. I will admit I need her as much as I need you to make me happy, but I am not trying to be selfish for any reason. I truly see this as the best situation for *all* of us."

"People are counting on me, Nico. I made vows when I became a deacon. I promised celibacy and obedience to God."

"Why would you do that? Let them count on someone else who actually *feels* the call to be a priest. I'm shocked that Father Andrew would even consider making you agree to something you have no desire to do. The life of a priest is all about sacrifice and solitude. It's a hard life, and one that comes with a lot of challenges. You have to want to serve God above anything, and I don't see that passion in you. I never have. Plenty of lay people are deeply religious, but they don't all choose a life of serving the congregation and turning their backs on their own physical and emotional needs. You're too grounded in your human cravings to give them up."

"Nico…" Matty sighed.

"I want you to do something for me," Nico said. "I want you to imagine for a moment what it would be like to have a beautiful wife like Eden and the gorgeous, brilliant children you could make with her."

Matty couldn't look at Nico when he asked, "What if I turn out like my own father?"

"Is that what's worrying you?"

"Sometimes."

"Matthew Remington, never *ever* think that again. Look at how much you love my family. Look at how much you love *me* and how much you want to love Eden. You're a lover, not a destroyer. Furthermore, I can imagine you were plenty depressed at times. Were you ever tempted to steal the sacramental wine at the seminary and go on a drinking spree to drown yourself in oblivion?"

"Of course not."

"Have you ever been tempted to harm another person?"

"Not exactly, but I did strike my father."

"To save your own life! That doesn't mean you're a violent person. It means you have a normal sense of self-preservation. Look at how many times you tried to help him when he never deserved it. And look at how many times you took his beatings and didn't fight back."

"I was afraid of making the beatings worse if I tried!" Matty's chest heaved for a moment until he calmed himself. He said with his voice cracking, "He loved my mother, and he only turned mean when she was… gone. What if I lost you or lost Eden? Maybe I'd turn into a monster like he did."

"Look, Matty, you can 'what if' all day long. What if the city of Los Angeles burns down or the whole earth floods? What if, what if…? You can go on forever. Trust the *now*. Did you feel any kinship with the other seminarians? Could you relate to their beliefs? I ask this because Eden had a difficult time understanding her fellow nursing students until she accepted that she was different from them and had different goals. It was only then that she started to make friends and enjoy their company. Did you ever feel as if you belonged at seminary with the other men?"

"Hmm… not really. I ended up spending a lot of my time alone or reading. And one of the priests taught me a little about boxing, so I would blow off steam punching a bag now and then."

"Not surprising, and the boxing accounts for how you look now. Did you pray a lot?"

"I was supposed to, and I tried to, but it wasn't very satisfactory. I was too angry most of the time. Or sad. My prayers became all jumbled up like I wanted to argue with God."

"Are you less angry and sad here in this house with me?"

This time Matty looked straight into Nico's eyes and answered, "Yes. Without a doubt."

Nico smiled gently. "I think it's time you have a serious talk with Father Andrew. I'll be there with you if you need me. You cannot go through with final vows, Matty. You just can't."

"Maybe you're right." Matty hung his head. "Maybe after my father passes and I can settle his estate, I can pay back the diocese. I just don't know what, if anything, is left besides the house. For all I know, he's squandered everything, and maybe that's why the servants left."

"If you can't pay them, I'll help."

"It's my problem, and I can't ask you to do that. Besides,

you're just starting out. I can't believe you are rolling in riches."

"We'll figure it out together. Your problem is my problem. I love you. Remember?"

"You loved me as a boy, Nico. Maybe I've changed. And you have Eden and a baby to take care of."

"Don't worry about Eden. I'll never stop loving her and making her a priority. She'll want you too. And I don't believe that the boy I knew would have somehow become anything other than an outstanding man."

Just then, Suzette came into the library and told them, "Your beautiful Eden has reached her limit today, I am afraid. She has gone to lie down until we have dinner. Your fathers will be home in a couple of hours, so perhaps you also need a little rest, hmm? This has been a very emotional day for everyone."

"Thank you, Maman. Perhaps you're right."

She left before seeing Nico take Matty's hand and lead him down the hall.

EDEN HAD NEVER FELT SO EXHAUSTED IN HER LIFE. HER HEAD was swimming with emotions and questions for Nico, but her tiredness completely got the best of her. Suzette recognized her need to lie down and told her, "This is quite normal in early pregnancy. Your body needs to get used to its new passenger." This made Eden smile, as she took her leave and headed for Nico's room. Suzette and Marguerite had shown her some beautiful fabric and styles she'd never have considered for herself. Like so many other things she'd experienced since she entered Nico's childhood home, the new designs opened up a world of imagination for Eden.

Eden wondered, however, if Suzette and Marguerite had been more concerned with convincing her to accept Matty into her life along with Nico than they had been in discussing fashion. She was thankful for their counsel, and without a doubt they'd bolstered her confidence. They certainly gave her a lot to think about, and that was far more important than worrying about pretty dresses.

Too much to think about right now, she complained to herself as she removed her dress and shoes. In her light underthings, she climbed into Nico's bed wearily and was sound asleep in less than a minute.

An hour later she awoke because she felt terribly warm. Nico's arm was draped across her middle, and she smiled sleepily at it. But... *when did the hair on Nico's arm turn black? Oh, there it is,* she realized. His arm with golden hair was flung across her parallel to the other one. *What?* Someone was snoring softly on either side of her. She sat up suddenly and looked to her right and then her left. Nico and Matty were waking up slowly and confusedly as if from a trance. She wanted to be angry because *they should have asked first, for heaven's sake*, but she found herself giggling uncontrollably instead.

"What possessed the two of you to climb into bed with me like this?" she asked once she could manage a straight face.

"Sorry my sweetest. You looked so peaceful and gorgeous, and we knew you needed the rest. We didn't want to wake you," Nico explained. "Your tiredness overtook us too. It's been such an emotional day, we couldn't help it. We've all had very little sleep."

"Well," Eden tried to look put out and failed miserably. "I must admit, it's a rather splendid feeling to be blanketed by the two of you like this."

"I'm sure we could make it even better…" Nico started.

Matty interrupted, "I can leave. I'm sorry."

Eden gently took hold of his arm and told him, "No. Please stay. I think I understand Nico's need for you better now. Somehow, I feel… balanced when you're near me. I never thought anything was missing, but I see now that we may have been incomplete."

"This is wonderful news," Nico beamed.

"I'm not making any promises," she answered quickly. "I still want to make sure that Matty isn't going to drive a wedge between us or that I'm less important to you than I believed earlier."

The men both sat up beside her and scooted back so they could lean against the headboard of the large bed. Nico looked seriously into her eyes as he stroked her hand.

Matty, on the other hand, looked longingly at her pert breasts with her rosy nipples visible through her sheer under-garment, but he kept his mouth shut and forced himself to keep his hands to himself.

"Matty was the most important person to me—besides my parents—for a long time. I love him with my whole heart, and I have made love to him."

"I thought you said I was your first!" Eden protested.

"I'm sorry I misled you. I told you that you were the first woman I'd made love to, and that was the truth."

"Splitting hairs," she grumbled and narrowed her eyes at him.

"Perhaps. Matty is my past and my future, I hope. But when I thought that he was lost to me forever, I met you, and you also became my true love. I never lost the feelings I had for Matty even as I realized how deeply I loved you, Eden. My heart has an infinite capacity, and I know that I will love our children with just as much depth. Look at my parents if you need confirmation that this is possible. Ask them questions. But mostly believe me. I love you deeply and forever, and I love Matty. I can't choose one or the other of you because you're like extensions of me now. You see how perfect it feels to be surrounded by Matty and me? We can surround your heart that way as well. I see you beginning to accept Matty, and that makes me as happy as when you agreed to marry me. I know how special you are, and you will learn how special Matty is if he can ever get his thinking straightened out enough to do the right thing." He looked at Matty then and saw his riveted attention on Eden's chest. "Matty? Are you listening?"

Tearing his eyes away and giving himself a little shake, Matty began. "I… I just don't know how to do this. I don't know if I trust myself enough, and I don't know if I can extricate myself from the bonds of the church."

"We'll help," Eden whispered. She too had noticed Matty's drifting attention, so she gently took his hand and placed it over her breast, causing him to give a small gasp. "If this is so important to Nico, then I can't break his heart. I can see how strong your convictions are, Matty, and that speaks well of your character. I'm still reeling from all that I've heard today, but it's starting to feel right." She looked down at his hand and grinned. "Especially now." Capturing his gaze, she said, "Perhaps you and I should spend some time getting to know one another—whether it's with Nico or without him, and… we'll see."

There was a knock on the door before anyone could respond to her statement. It was Suzette asking, "Pardon me, is Matty in there? Father Andrew has apparently been looking for him and sent a nun to see if he was here. She would like Matty to accompany her back to Father Andrew's office."

"Yes. He'll be right out," Nico answered for him. "Thank you, Maman."

Matty looked down at himself and whispered, "Oh. I'm

not sure I can walk very well just yet." He reluctantly dropped his hand from Eden's breast.

Missing the feel of him but seeing the tent in his trousers, Eden said softly, "Oh!"

Nico looked at Matty and smiled knowingly. "Oh."

Matty gave a tiny groan and slowly got off the bed. He put his shirt and shoes back on silently—looking anywhere but at Eden.

As Matty turned toward the door, Nico said seriously, "I assume your father has passed, and Father Andrew wants to tell you in person. I'm sorry. Even despite all the trouble you've had with him, this must hurt on some level. Do you want me or both of us to come with you?"

"Thank you, but I think I'd rather face this on my own. I'll be in touch." He gave Nico a quick kiss and paused a split second before also giving one to Eden. And then he left.

Matty did not make it back to dinner that night, nor did he climb in through Nico's window. Nico slept poorly, half-expecting Matty to appear during the night. He was alert at the slightest sound, hoping it would be Matty coming home. But nothing happened.

Prior to his sleeplessness, however, he and Eden made good use of their time in bed together. He shared things he knew about sex with three people and told her the kind of lover Matty was, making her get hot and bothered at the idea. Done talking at last, he kissed and licked her pleasure center over and over until she shook with a satisfying climax. When he finally entered her, he also invaded her backside with two well-lubricated fingers and whispered in her ear, "Pretend that my hand is Matty. Can you imagine having both of us inside you at the same time, rubbing against one another, and filling you with our love?" That was enough to put Eden over the top once again as she moaned both of their names in ecstasy. Nico could not stop grinning until his pleasure became so intense that he grimaced and poured into her.

Thirteen

OVER BREAKFAST THE NEXT MORNING, NICO ASKED HIS mother, "Are you certain Sister Mary Gertrude didn't say anything else about why Father Andrew wanted Matty to come to his office?"

"I am quite sure, Nicolo. The little nun was so skittish she could barely look at me, and only asked if I knew of Matty's whereabouts because Father Andrew wanted him immediately. I promise you that was all."

"It's so odd that he didn't return. I'm going to head over to his house and find out what happened. If he's not there, I'll go to the church." He looked at Eden and said, "Why don't you stay and relax, and hopefully I'll be back soon—maybe even with Matty. But if I can find Father Andrew too, I'll talk to him about a wedding."

"I guess I can wait here, but isn't there anything I can do?"

"Why don't you spend the time thinking about how you want to get married and getting to know my mother better? At some point, we'll want to find our own place to live, so take advantage of her company while you can."

Suzette spoke up, "We can definitely talk about wedding plans, Nicolo. I will take care of your Eden. But do not be gone long. She may become bored with my company."

Eden chuckled. "Never."

Rising from the table, Nico added, "I also need to talk to Doc Louis soon about starting back to work at the clinic."

With a concerned expression, Eden said, "If you're leaving right now, I'll see you to the door." They made their way out of the dining room and out of earshot before she asked, "Mentioning Doc Louis brought up another of my concerns, and I would rather ask you about it privately." She looked down and gathered her thoughts while Nico stared at her. Facing him, she asked quietly, "How badly do you want me to work in the clinic? That isn't one of the main reasons you asked me to marry you, is it?"

Nico's eyebrows shot up. "Eden, no! Of course it isn't. Remember I said you could choose to work there or not, and it was completely up to you. While I would welcome your company and think you might want to utilize the skills you learned in nursing school, I also think you may be less interested in a strenuous job while you're pregnant. If it were all up to me, I would honestly prefer that you *didn't* work in the clinic—or if you wanted to be there in some capacity, perhaps you could take on something physically easy to handle. I want to make sure you stay healthy. There are lots of jobs that are probably unsuitable for a pregnant woman. I hope you haven't been fretting about it or thinking that I wanted to take advantage of you in some way."

"Not really. I'm convinced you love me, but I worry sometimes and just wanted to be certain. The truth is, I don't think I have the energy to do much work. Maybe that will get better with time. I don't want to be in the way or be a detriment to your medical practice."

Nico pulled Eden into his arms and kissed the top of her head. "How about this? You made some friends at your school, so maybe you can think of one or two of them you'd like to offer the job to. Surely with the dedicated ladies you studied with, there is someone suitable and hardworking you think would enjoy living in Los Angeles. Why don't you write some letters and see who might be interested?"

"Oh, Nico, I think *most* of them are interested in finding jobs. The employment prospects for those women aren't at all promising, so if you could provide jobs for a couple of them, that would be wonderful. I'll write some letters right away. Thank you." She stood on her tiptoes and planted a kiss on his lips. "Good luck finding Matty. I hope everything is right with him."

"Have I told you today how much I love your smile, Eden?" He gave her another hug.

"You just did. Now go find our man and bring him back to us."

"And I love how this attitude of yours is developing." He kissed her and was off.

Eden turned back toward the dining room where Suzette was saying goodbye to her husbands who were ready to head off to work. Walter was dressed in an impeccably tailored suit, and Isaac wore clean but casual work clothes. He was telling them about an order he'd received to make instruments for a Boston music school. Besides designing and building fabulous furniture, Isaac was a talented and sought-after luthier. This was all new to Eden, who had not been around musicians before.

Isaac said, "I finally have all of the wood I need to complete the order. It's going to be a rewarding job to do."

"That sounds so interesting," Eden exclaimed.

"Would you like to see the studio where I make them?"

"Oh, I would. Thank you."

"It's just a five-minute walk from here. We have all of the businesses together in one area. You can see what we all do if you like. Suzette, darling, why don't you come too, and then you ladies can walk home together? I have a new violin I'd love to show you. Maybe you'd like to try it out."

"Absolutely! We can be ready shortly," Suzette answered, looking at Eden.

Not long after that, Isaac was proudly showing Eden around his special studio reserved just for instrument making.

When he finished the tour, he pulled a shiny new violin off the wall, tuned it quickly, and grabbed a bow. He launched into a sweet piece of music that caused Eden's jaw to drop.

"What is that?" she whispered to Suzette.

"Mozart," Suzette replied almost reverently. "Oh, Isaac, the tone is magnificent."

Isaac stopped playing and handed the instrument and bow off to Suzette. She played a couple scales, grinned, and then launched into something else, nodding to Isaac. He picked up another violin and seamlessly joined her.

Eden looked questioningly at Walter who stood watching with stars in his eyes. He turned to Eden and proclaimed, "This is a Haydn duet they play sometimes to warm up." He sighed. "I am the luckiest man in the world."

While the music was pretty, it wasn't something Eden could say she adored. But the piece drew to a finish, and Isaac put down his instrument, saying, "Go on, Suzette, show Eden what you can do."

Suzette launched into a piece that looked impossible. Her fingers and the bow danced over the strings as the most amazing sounds Eden had ever imagined poured out of the violin. There wasn't a sound in the building except for her music. The men in the next room even stopped their work and approached the door to watch and enjoy. This was music like nothing Eden had ever imagined, and Suzette was creating it!

When she was finished and took a modest bow to every-one's applause, Isaac explained, "That composition was written by an old friend and mentor of Suzette's, Nicolo Paganini—the most famous violinist ever. We named Nicolo after him." He laughed. "Such irony."

"Oh my," was all Eden could say. "Thank you."

Briskly, Walter announced, "Ladies, Isaac, I must get going or I'll be late for my meeting. Thank you for the wonderful treat, as always." He planted a kiss on Isaac's and then Suzette's lips and rushed off.

Isaac too looked as if he was anxious to get back to work, so Eden and Suzette headed for home. It was a glorious sunny day, and Suzette waved and greeted several people along the way. A couple of times she introduced neighbors to Eden, explaining that the younger woman was Nicolo's fiancée. Everyone had something nice to say. Eden couldn't believe how lovely everything was.

She knew how Walter felt. Perhaps she was the luckiest woman in the world.

WHILE EDEN WAS BECOMING ACCUSTOMED TO THE TALENTS OF Nico's family, Nico was having a long chat with Matty. He'd discovered his friend at the Remington residence looking lost and troubled.

Matty explained, "I went to see Father Andrew at his office at the church, and he confirmed that he went with the intent to give my pa the last rites. He chastised me again for not going with him, of course. Anyway, he said he was all prepared to administer the last rites, but when he arrived at the clinic, my father was sitting up in bed happily drinking a cup of coffee and eating a piece of pie."

"Why did Doc Louis think he was on death's door then?" Nico asked with a frown. He'd never known Doc Louis to be so wrong about something, but he figured there was a first time for everything. He hoped Doc Louis wasn't slipping in his old age. It wasn't all that difficult to identify when a person who was already critical was about to pass.

"I guess my pa was unconscious and breathing irregularly, so Doc Louis sent for Father Andrew. While Father Andrew was on his way there, however, Pa woke up and looked a lot better. Father Andrew told me that Doc Louis said he'd never seen anything like it. Said Pa was asking for something to eat and drink. So Doc Louis poured him some coffee and gave him the pie from his own lunch. Then Father Andrew arrived, and Doc Louis told him Pa was looking well enough to go home the next day. Father Andrew said a prayer for him and headed back to his office. Father Andrew was even madder at me about that, saying I'd missed my chance to make amends with my pa for once and for all. An hour later, Doc Louis showed up at the church office and said the old man finished his food, lay back, and died. He never got last rites after all."

"I'm sorry, Matty."

"So am I. The mean old coot didn't even get to repent or to be absolved."

"I guess you have a funeral to plan now, don't you?"

"I'm keeping it as simple as possible. I've made arrangements for tomorrow afternoon."

"Is that why you didn't come back to the house?"

"Only partly. It was more because Father Andrew and I got into a big argument. After he stormed out of his office saying he had better things to do than argue with a spoiled, ungrateful brat, I wasn't feeling terribly sociable. I didn't want to bring my troubles to your family dinner. So I came back here and tried unsuccessfully to sleep. When I couldn't do that, I started cleaning up around the house. I've been up most of the night."

"Matty, you know my parents and I wouldn't have cared, no matter when you showed up or in what state. And Eden and I would like to be there for you when you need support. But what did you two argue about that put you in such a bad mood?"

"You can imagine. After he told me what a horrible son I was and how I should have been there for my father's last moments alive no matter how he'd treated me, I offered to pay back the diocese for my tuition, and he wouldn't hear of it. He said I have a much bigger debt to pay than the monetary investment they made in me." Matty's voice broke as he finished speaking.

"Matty, before we get into this any further, did you have anything to eat last night?"

"Oh, um, no."

"And this morning?"

Matty shook his head.

"Come with me right now. We're heading back to my parents' house so we can feed you. I don't want you making yourself sick. Let's go. Or—wait a moment. Go pack up whatever belongings you need, and let's get you out of this house for good. It can't be healthy for you to be here right now alone. You need to be around the people who love you. My parents and Eden would never forgive me if I let you stay here alone."

Matty could hardly disagree, and the thought of being around the people who were far more of a family to him than his own made his heart swell. He was also lightheaded with hunger.

On the way to the Stark-James estate, Matty explained more of his thinking. "If my father was that sick, even if he'd taken a turn for the better, I don't understand why he wasn't given last rites anyway. It was inevitable that he was going to die, and it's not as if a priest can only give them one time if there's been a misjudgment. There is something about this whole story that doesn't add up."

"I agree. I'll have a chat with Doc Louis as soon as possible. Eating pie and then dying? I think I'll ring him up and ask when we get home."

They arrived at the Stark-James household. Matty had just stowed his meager belongings in Nico's room when the ladies reappeared. Matty confirmed that his father had passed, so both Suzette and Eden smothered him in warm hugs.

"You are looking terribly gaunt, my sweet boy," Suzette muttered as she patted his cheek. "We will take care of you." Suzette then left to order up something substantial for Matty to eat.

Soon they were seated in the dining room where Suzette piled Matty's plate with a huge amount of food and encouraged Eden to nibble on a few things because she too was looking pale.

Nico excused himself then and said, "I need to make a call to Doc Louis."

While Matty stuffed his face like a starving man, Eden nibbled on some slices of ripe peach and a piece of sponge cake. No one spoke much because Matty was in such a feeding frenzy. The ladies thought they would let him be.

Nico returned in a few minutes with a strange look on his face. He poured himself some coffee from the sideboard and sat down with a plunk, saying, "Something isn't right."

Matty looked up from his food and raised his eyebrows.

"Father Andrew is lying."

"Nico!" admonished Suzette.

"Hear me out, Maman. He's telling a different story than what Doc Louis had to say, and I would trust Doc Louis with my life. Father Andrew has a possible ulterior motive, and it would not be the first time he'd bent the truth to suit himself. I don't know why he told Matty that his pa didn't receive last rites or some cock-and-bull story about getting better momentarily and then dropping dead. But he did say all of that. Doc Louis is on his way over right now to speak to Matty personally." He looked at Matty. "He apologized for not reaching out to you sooner, but he had an emergency to deal with."

"Thanks, Nico."

"This is very strange. I'm glad your fathers are on their way home soon for lunch to hear this," Suzette mused.

Doc Louis arrived at roughly the same time as Isaac and Walter, and soon Doc Louis' story began to pour out as everyone had their noon meal—and Matty had dessert. "I summoned Father Andrew with instructions that Mr. Remington was about to breathe his last and to hurry. He took his time, however, and I thought he had ignored me, but he finally wandered in full of chit chat about the fine weather and whatnot. He did not seem to be trying to hurry at all. Finally, after I pointed out that Mr. Remington was barely breathing, he said some words over him in Latin that I did not understand. Mr. Remington passed away while the priest was praying. Was it last rites? I assume so. Why would he not give them to a man who was clearly dying? I have seen him do this with other terminal patients, and this didn't seem to be anything different. I have just never seen him act so nonchalantly that he could not finish before the patient expired. Does that matter, Matty?"

"Technically, it does, but I guess it's not crucial if he did his best. What was this business about my pa sitting up and eating a piece of pie from your lunch before he dropped dead?"

"What? I do not take pie into the clinic to eat. That is absurd. And the man's heart was barely beating. He could not have sat up and eaten anything. What kind of nonsense is this?"

Isaac spoke up and asked, "Not to change the subject but,

Matty, what are your feelings about taking your final vows? Do you actually want to become a priest?"

"I'm not sure, sir, that I know exactly what to do. Father Andrew has made it clear that he expects it of me. But deep in my heart, no. I do not want to be a priest for the rest of my life." He looked at Nico and then at Eden. "I want to follow my heart for once, but I can't find a way out of the snare I'm trapped in."

"Well, that is simply wrong!" Walter spluttered. When Matty's head jerked, he instantly clarified, "You need to make your *own* destiny, my boy. We'll just have to work out a way for you to make Father Andrew see that he's made a colossal mistake. And I do apologize if our previous efforts in getting you to safety had a deleterious effect on your life. It was our intent for you to spend a couple of years away at boarding school out of your father's clutches, and then return here to live where you wanted—most likely with us—until you determined what you wanted to do. We never expected you to be hidden away in some remote seminary where you were forced into the priesthood against your will." He looked around at his family. "We will need to form a united front and see to it that you get your way. Father Andrew doesn't own you. That kind of nonsense was abolished many years ago."

"I have offered to pay back the diocese, but he refused to let me, and besides, I don't even know if I have any money."

"Matty, don't even dream about worrying about money,"

Isaac assured him. "You have always been like part of this family, and we can help."

"I can't ask that of you."

Nico spoke up, "You didn't. We've had this conversation, Matty. You're as good as part of this family, and we take care of our own."

"Well, even if you paid the diocese and I could sell the house and pay you back, Father Andrew said he wouldn't let that happen."

"We shall see about that," Walter said in a steely tone. "Father Andrew answers to the diocese—he doesn't control them, so you ought to speak to them yourself." He smiled gently. "Now why don't the three of you all go lie down for a while? Eden is yawning, and Matty, you look like you haven't slept in days. Everything will work itself out. Don't worry."

Doc Louis winked at Nico and said, "We will chat later about the clinic. You look like you could use a nap too, young man."

"Yes sir." Nico offered his hand to Eden, and they stood to go.

Matty turned around before exiting the dining room and said, "Once again, I can't thank you enough. You all mean so much to me."

As soon as they reached Nico's room at the other end of the house, their lethargy dissipated, and clothes began to fall away. Nico nearly ripped off his own and then began to help Eden out of hers. Matty plopped himself into a chair and removed his shoes slowly as he watched the disrobing eagerly. Unbuttoning his shirt, he watched as Nico's naked body gleamed in the filtered light that came through the curtains. His manhood stood out proud from his body as he assisted Eden out of one layer after another. When Eden stood before him unashamedly nude, Matty thought he might swallow his tongue. He'd never seen so much beautiful flesh all at once, and when both of them faced him, he began to shake.

"Stand up, Matty. Please," she said.

Matty unbuttoned his trousers and stood, letting them sag around his hips.

Eden smiled at him and turned back to Nico. "I have no idea what to do, but I have a strong sense that Matty needs us to take care of him right now. Can you help me make him feel better?"

Nico groaned into her neck. "I love you so much, Eden. Of course. You're fine with this?"

"Yes. Your mother and Marguerite convinced me that I would be a terribly lucky woman if I had the attention of the two of you. They did not have to spend too much time persuading me."

"My mother told you that, eh?" Nico asked with a low laugh. "Interesting conversation, was it?"

"Most interesting. They offered to give specific advice should I ever want to talk, but so far it was just encouragement."

"The ladies know what they're talking about, I'm sure."

Nico turned back to Matty and helped divest him of the rest of his clothes. "Isn't our man beautiful, Eden?" He grinned at her. "Kiss him, please."

As soon as Eden's lips found Matty's, he sought her breast with one hand and reached around to grasp her buttock with the other, groaning with pleasure the whole time. Nico stepped behind Matty and stroked his body all over. Then he reached around Matty for Eden's hand and placed it on Matty's stiff cock. She hummed a pleasant little sound as Nico encouraged her hand to stroke Matty's length in tandem with his hand. His own cock was notched between Matty's buttocks where he stroked up and down rhythmically. Matty's breath sped up. "Not so tired now, are you?" Nico teased.

Matty smiled. He released Eden's mouth and said, "I *know* I shouldn't be doing this, but I find I'm powerless to stop." Then he lowered his lips to her breast. He began to swirl her nipple with his tongue and then nipped her a few times. Eden firmed up her grasp on his cock.

Whispering into Matty's ear, Nico asked, "You've never tasted a woman, have you? It gives Eden extreme pleasure to be on the receiving end of that, and it's terribly exciting to do."

Matty straightened up and said, "Show me."

Eden lay down and patted the bed next to her. "Come lie next to me, Matty." She opened her legs, making room for Nico who immediately took advantage of her position. He reached between her legs and groaned.

"She's already so wet and anxious for us, Matty. Give me your hand." Together their fingers probed her, and Nico showed Matty how to make swirling motions around her clit. He then told Matty, "Keep fucking her with your fingers while I do this with my mouth, and you'll see our beautiful Eden come apart with profound pleasure."

It only took a minute or two. Eden began squirming and panting as Matty's two fingers probed in and out and Nico sucked and licked at her pleasure center. When her moans grew louder, Nico pulled back and told Matty, "Suck on this little nub right here. She'll love it."

Matty leaned in and did as he was told. He'd given Nico this kind of pleasure many times, so he figured he'd use his mouth in roughly the same way. A moment later he was supremely gratified to watch Eden climax.

She grasped both of the men and let out a long cry of bliss as she toppled over the edge of sublime sensation. Nico and Matty grinned at each other.

"Now put your cock in her. She'll love that as well," Nico commanded. "I'll take care of you at the same time."

"You mean…?"

Nico nodded to him.

"I thought I might never get to experience that again." Matty shivered with anticipation and lowered himself into Eden's body. She helped guide him in as his eyes grew wide. "Oh my God. This must be heaven." Eden's wet warmth engulfed his cock, and he realized this couldn't possibly compare to the feeling of his or Nico's hand stroking him. That was pleasure, but this was perfection. It was a gift. He had to hold himself still for a moment just to appreciate the sensation.

Eden smiled and whispered, "Oh, Matty, you feel so perfect." She pulled him down for a kiss.

Nico picked up a towel and a small cruet of oil someone had left on the bedside table. Apparently, his parents wanted to ensure everyone's comfort. He took a moment to appreciate the beauty of his lovers making love to one another, and the vision of them made him incredibly hard. Carefully, he drizzled some oil into his hand and coated his own cock with it, then gently began to oil Matty's backside. He kissed Matty's buttocks and slowly penetrated him, first with one and then two of his oily fingers.

With his chest heaving, Matty made an ungodly sound that emanated from deep within him as Nico's stiff cock breached his hole. Both men let out matching groans of pleasure as Nico entered and retreated in small increments.

When Matty felt relaxed enough, Nico grabbed his hips and plunged into him to the hilt. Matty's head jerked back with his eyes closed in concentration. "This is incredible!" he cried. "I'm making love to both of you at the same time."

Nico took over the tempo as he pumped in and out of Matty, causing Matty to drive in and out of Eden at the same pace. He then released Matty's hip with one hand and reached for Eden's clit. In moments, she was shuddering through another climax, causing ripples of pleasure to pour through Matty as her muscles contracted around him. Harder and harder, Nico pounded into Matty from behind until Matty couldn't take the pleasure anymore. He growled and spilled his seed into Eden. Then Nico changed his angle, hitting something special inside of him, and Matty howled as another wave of extreme pleasure overtook his senses. He nearly collapsed onto Eden, but Nico grabbed both Matty's hips again and drilled him, grinding against his butt, as Nico let out a nearly primal moan and emptied himself into Matty.

Eden watched all of this with a beautiful smile gracing her lovely face. "You're both incredible," she whispered. "My heart has never felt this full."

As they all flopped down beside one another, legs and arms jumbled together, Matty said, "If I ever had a thought about spending the rest of my life celibate, that notion is definitely banished now. Thank you both for your love."

"You have it forever, you know," Nico murmured against Matty's throat.

Eden curled up even closer to him and fell asleep. Matty was close behind.

Nico took a moment to wipe things up with the towel and then pulled the bedclothes over them and also went to sleep. His last conscious thought was, "Finally!"

Fifteen

NICO WAS THE FIRST TO AWAKEN. HE CAREFULLY EXTRICATED himself so as not to disturb the others. Looking at Eden and Matty together made his heart warm. They were so perfect—and all his.

He had an idea, so he quickly washed up and dressed, leaving the room quietly as he went off to find Suzette.

Half an hour later, he returned with an armload of items he and his mother had located.

Matty was just beginning to stir as Nico placed a stack of shirts, jackets, and trousers on the chair by the bed. Rubbing his eyes and yawning, Matty asked quietly, "What's all this?"

"Just a few things to make you feel more… conventional. You can have anything you like. No one is using these. Maman and I ransacked the wardrobes in Bay and Warren's rooms looking for clothes they'd left behind." While Nico was tall, Warren and Bay were built more like Isaac with his great height and broad chest. These items were things they'd outgrown but were still nice. Nico would have shared his own clothes with Matty, but he needed what he had and probably ought to acquire more for himself anyway.

"Maman also wanted me to tell you that she sent word to Father Andrew, inviting him to dinner tonight. If he doesn't show up, maybe we can speak to him after the funeral tomorrow."

"We? Nico, this is my problem. You don't need to trouble yourself."

"Matty, my entire family has promised to do whatever it takes to help you make this situation right. You heard Papa. He feels terrible that they unwittingly subjected you to Father Andrew's warped idea of what ought to happen to you. I agree with your assessment that the man is a lot more ambitious and devious than anyone expected. So accept my family's help and stop worrying about it. Now, go get yourself cleaned up and try on some of these clothes. I'd love to see you in something other than black."

SUZETTE'S INVITATION TO DINNER WENT UNANSWERED BY Father Andrew—unusual for a man with a rather famous appetite. Either he had some ecclesiastical emergency, or he was avoiding them.

He did not send his regrets.

Stranger still, Father Andrew also did not show up the next day for Mr. Remington's funeral. He left word with Sister Mary Gertrude that Matty was perfectly capable of handling it on his own. This forced Matty to rush back and change into his clerical collar and black clothes.

Father Andrew's actions—whatever their motive—erased any patience Matty had left. The decision to force him to lead the funeral prayers for his own father was the last straw; he was ready to quit this charade.

"Whoever heard of a man of the cloth having to officiate a funeral for a member of his own family?" Walter spluttered at Isaac upon hearing the news. "This is heartless and highly irregular."

Isaac shook his head, clearly in agreement with his husband.

At the chapel, the Stark-James family made up the entire roster of attendees with the notable exception of one man who looked as if he may have had a few drinks with Remington in the past. The worn, thin man stayed only long enough to see the coffin lowered into the grave and left without extending condolences to Matty. No one spoke any kind words over the grave extolling the man's accomplishments, his love for his family, or what a great friend he'd been. Matty merely said the requisite prayers, and that was it. To say it was a somber affair was putting it mildly.

At the gravesite, a messenger arrived with a note for

Matty. It was a directive from Mr. Remington's lawyer instructing Matty to come to his office as soon as possible. Once again, Walter took umbrage with this and exclaimed, "Doesn't anyone in this town have the slightest respect for the sanctity of a funeral?"

The only bright spot was a bouquet of flowers Suzette had cut from their garden. She divided the blooms and placed half on the top of the coffin. The other half she laid on Mrs. Remington's grave. Before they left the cemetery, Matty kissed his fingers and placed them on his mother's headstone. He knelt in the grass for a moment—either praying silently or thinking. No one bothered him. But when he rose, Eden and Nico took his arms and walked him to the cemetery gate.

"Do you want us to go with you to see the lawyer?" Nico asked.

"No, thank you. You don't need to waste your time with that. I'll see you back at your house as soon as I'm finished with him."

It was several hours before Matty arrived back at the estate. This time he carried another valise that looked rather heavy. The heaviest thing about him, however, was the look in his eyes.

Everyone gathered in the parlor to hear what Matty had to report.

CHAPTER
Sixteen

"As you know, I had a meeting with Pa's lawyer, and to put things as succinctly as possible, I am completely penniless. Apparently, my father had no idea how to manage his finances despite several suggestions from his lawyer. He used up his inheritance by living beyond his means for quite some time, and the reason most of the servants left was because he refused to pay them. A couple of them stayed on for the free lodging for a while, but even that became too difficult for them—no surprise, considering how tough it was to live with my father—and they left to find employment elsewhere.

"When I was cleaning the house a few days ago, I did not go through such things as my mother's jewelry or the silver—and avoided my father's study—but now I find that anything of particular value has been either confiscated or traded to creditors. The property itself is to be auctioned off in a few days. I was told to go through the house and retrieve any personal items I saw fit to keep, and the rest would be used to pay off my father's astronomical debts. I'm sure his lawyer expects his fee to come from that as well.

"So I picked out a couple of framed daguerreotypes of my family—one of all of us and a beautiful one of my mother. And I located an old chess set that my pa taught me to play with before…" He stopped and cleared his throat, looking out the window.

Everyone knew that "before" meant before his father started drinking excessively and behaving like a madman.

"I find it is comforting to have something to help me remember that my family life wasn't always terrible. Now, if you'll all excuse me, I'd like to have a moment to myself."

Suzette stood before Matty could make it to the door, wrapped him in a motherly hug, and said, "Matty, we are all terribly sorry for all that you are dealing with. Please remember always how much we love you in this family." Matty gave her a sad smile as she said, "Now… would you consider setting the chessboard up in the library where everyone can enjoy it? I have always found them quite beautiful."

"Would you teach me to play?" Eden asked with a hopeful smile.

"Yes, thank you. I can do that." Matty forced a smile and

nodded to them all before shuffling out of the room with the heavy case in tow.

"This has been a dreadful day for that poor fellow," Walter observed. "We need to cheer him up."

Isaac looked kindly at Walter and said, "Let him be for a while. He needs to grieve more than he probably realizes. He'll come around. At least he knows he's loved in this house."

Isaac knew a thing or two about paralyzing grief. Walter put his arm around Isaac's broad shoulders and squeezed.

With Matty gone, Suzette looked at Eden and asked, "Eden, darling, have you given any more thought to when and how you'd like to be married? And you as well, Nicolo? How will this affect Matty?"

"We haven't discussed it much yet, Maman, and certainly not with Matty. We've just managed to bring him around to accepting us. It's only been a short time."

"I do still want to marry soon, though, Nico," Eden said. "If we could do it tomorrow, it would be fine with me." She looked at Suzette. "While Marguerite's dress designs are beautiful and having a fancy wedding might be exciting for some people, I'm actually only interested in the legality of the ceremony—not in having a fancy event. I'm not happy being the center of attention, I suppose. I don't mean to sound like an ingrate, but the expense would be wasted on me. Remember… I grew up in the sticks on an isolated ranch, and my parents wouldn't even want to take the time off to travel anywhere for the ceremony."

"How about this?" Nico asked. "You and I can take the train tomorrow like we planned. We'll go as far as Santa Ana, and from there we can hire a buggy to get to their ranch. I can ask your father properly for your hand in marriage. Then we can either marry there or come back to Los Angeles and marry with my family all here to help celebrate. I'd hate to make them miss out on an occasion to entertain, even if it's after a simple ceremony. So… I guess you know where I'd prefer to get married—if that is acceptable to you."

Eden's face glowed with happiness. "I like this plan very much. We'll do that. But what about Matty? How does he fit into our union? I'm fairly certain I can't tell my parents about him because they would never accept me being with two men. But he's so special and I know how much you love him. I don't want anything to cause more hurt for him with everything that's happened in his life lately." She turned to Nico's parents. "Excuse me for asking, but are you all legally married somehow? Nico told me about the San Francisco judge."

They all smiled, and Isaac laughed, saying, "Whether it's perfectly legal or not has never bothered us. We did what we could, and it meant something to us that we made the effort. That was what mattered. If Matty is up for the conversation, talk to him tonight. I like to see that you're considering his feelings so seriously. If you can't manage to arrange a marriage for all three of you, Eden, would you consider marrying Matty instead of Nicolo? You're already having Nicolo's baby, and that in itself ties you to him irrevocably forever." He took in their surprised expressions and added, "It's just a suggestion. Think it over. Another idea would be that Walter and I can look around and see if we could find a similar judge in Los Angeles who could be paid to marry all three of you."

Nico's eyes lit up, and he asked, "Do you think that would be possible, Pa?"

Isaac shrugged. "Eh, we know a fair number of people through our building company, so maybe if we all put our heads together, we can come up with someone to ask, but I wouldn't pin all your hopes on that, son. People in Los Angeles don't have the same sense of gold fever that was so prevalent back then in San Francisco—not to say there aren't folks who would do just about anything for some extra money."

"Would you see if you can find someone for the job while Eden and I are in Capistrano? We won't be gone for more than a day, I assume." He looked at Eden and added, "Unless you want to spend more time with your family. I don't mean to rush you. You haven't seen them in quite a long time."

"No, it's fine. I'd rather get back here and get married. We can visit again when it's not such a busy time of year for them."

"What is keeping them especially busy right now?" Walter

asked. He always wanted to learn new things, and cattle ranching was outside of his regular reading interests.

"It's the beginning of calving season, and everyone is helping with that as well as branding. It's a terribly hectic time. That's why my parents couldn't possibly plan a wedding or attend one." She looked at Nico and laughed softly. "They may even try to get you to help with calving in case one of the cows has a difficult birth."

Nico made a face. "Hmm. Cows are not exactly my specialty. Maybe I should send Matty with you instead. He can bless the heifers or something." He gave her a kiss on the cheek to let her know he was joking and announced to his parents, "We'll be back as soon as possible. I just want to go make a favorable impression and let them know that their daughter is deeply loved and will be well cared for."

"Walter and I will start asking around and see what we come up with, and your mother can arrange for a dinner party for the family and our closest friends. You just have a safe trip and don't worry about the logistics. Now, you'd better go find Matty and tell him your plans."

THEY WANDERED THROUGH THE HOUSE AND FINALLY FOUND Matty sitting outside in the interior courtyard. Facing away from them, he appeared deep in thought and was startled when they sat down on either side of him on his bench. Nico stretched his arm around Matty's shoulders and Eden took his hand. No one spoke for a while; they just sat quietly enjoying the flowers.

Finally, Nico explained to Matty that they planned to travel to the Godwin ranch the next day, and they would love to have Matty come if he wished. He also mentioned Isaac's suggestion that Matty might marry Eden instead of him. It was hard to read Nico's expression when he said that.

"Absolutely not," Matty said with finality. "I don't mean to be insulting to you in any way, Eden. I think you're a wonderful woman, and I would be honored to be your husband, but to show up at your parents' place and announce, 'Here I am asking for your daughter's hand, but don't mind that I have no money, no job prospect, and in marrying her, I'm breaking the vows I'm supposed to be taking to become a priest, thereby destroying any chance I have to complete the job I have trained for.' How do you think they'd receive all of that information? They'd probably laugh… or shoot me."

Nico smiled gently. "It was just a suggestion for how to include you in our union. If Eden married you, I would still consider myself a full partner in the marriage. This baby is mine, so I'll always be wed to her in that regard anyway."

"All the more reason the two of you need to marry. I've been thinking that either I need to accept that I'm supposed to be a priest and seek a lot of absolution before I'm ordained, or I need to leave Los Angeles. Maybe it would be better if I made a fresh start somewhere else."

Eden gasped his name and squeezed his hand, and Nico nearly shouted, "No! You can't leave! Don't you remember how you felt when we were apart? It killed me inside, and I am pretty sure it was just as difficult for you, Matty. Why would you even suggest leaving?"

"You know why, Nico. I'm afraid I'll ruin what you and Eden have together, and I'll be a terrible influence around your child. I don't know how to be a father. I'm not even a good son, according to Father Andrew."

Eden scooted closer to Matty and took his hand in both of hers. "I can't believe you'd even worry about that. I see so much capacity for love in you. None of us know yet how to be a parent, and it's scary to think about. But this baby would be lucky to have two fathers the way Nico and his siblings did. He or she will learn that love is not limiting, it's infinite. Please don't leave us, Matty. We need you to be whole."

"I don't know what I'm doing! On one hand, I can't stand the idea of celibacy—especially now that I've been with the two of you. But if I don't become a priest, I have no other prospects for employment, and I can't keep sponging off of everyone. I've done too much of that already."

"You are not taking advantage of anyone. My family has made it clear that you are always welcome here and we all love you. Besides, we don't have to figure out everything all at once. You have the luxury now of being able to determine your own life's path. You don't have to follow in Father Andrew's footsteps just because he told you to. Matty, in all the years I've known you, you have always been a brilliant, inquisitive scholar, and I know you have deep faith, but I never—not even *once*—heard you consider the priesthood. It's not for you."

Matty's head dropped, and he studied his hand in Eden's. "You're right, of course. But that was when I was younger and unaware of my future inability to support myself any other way."

"So take some time and consider your options. You're so smart and well-educated, I'm sure you can find something that fulfills you more than a life of wearing heavy black clothes and listening to the ridiculous confessions of little old ladies in a stuffy booth."

Matty's head jerked up, and he looked at Nico flatly. "There is a lot more to being a priest than that, and you know it."

"Of course I do," he said softly and tightened his arm around Matty. "I also know that you would make a wonderful husband and father. Your pa had a problem, Matty. You're not him. And Father Andrew is manipulative. Don't cave in to his demands. We can figure something out to get him off your back, and you can figure out a great career for yourself. You're not going to end up on the streets because we refuse to let that happen. And you said yourself that you aren't cut out for a celibate life. Please don't worry so much. We love you." He leaned over and kissed the side of Matty's head.

Matty sighed and leaned into Nico. "You're right. I'm just

being emotional. I feel terrible that I'm not particularly sad about my pa passing, but in some ways, I guess I *am* actually sad. But only because we weren't able to make things right between us. I didn't try hard enough with him, and I regret that. But losing him also makes me miss my mother, even though she's been gone since I was quite young. I don't even know if I'm making any sense. Being around your family is comforting in a lot of ways, but in other ways it makes me feel even worse."

"Why worse?" Nico asked, confused.

"Just look at everyone. You all love each other so much, and you have so much joy in this house. Sometimes it's almost *too* much with the wonderful music and… well… it's perfect here."

Nico snorted. "You should have been here after you went away. My fathers were about to send me off to join the army just to get rid of me. I made everyone around me miserable."

"I seriously doubt that," Eden interjected.

"Believe it. Or ask them. They'll tell you I was a monster to live with for a while. It was only when I started working long hours in the clinic that I was finally too tired to bellyache all the time." Nico paused a second. "But my point is, yes, we love each other in this family, and we're proud of one another, but we're not perfect. Look at my brothers. Bay snores like a braying mule and Warren has smelly feet."

Eden giggled softly while Matty finally cracked a small smile.

"Matty, Eden and I are going to make the trip to the ranch a quick one. If you don't want to join us tomorrow, then use the time wisely and think about what you want to do. I'd talk to Papa, frankly. You know he's like a walking library, and he loves to share his opinions. Also, he and his business partners know practically every influential person in Los Angeles. Something wonderful will come up. I just know it. And later tonight, Eden and I can show you some more reasons for why you need to be with us forever."

"Absolutely," she agreed. "We just need to figure out how to get married and do it soon."

"I can marry you if that's what you'd like. I'm still a deacon, and that's something I have the authority to do."

Nico and Eden looked at each other questioningly. Finally, Nico answered, "Matty, we want you to marry *us*. Not *marry* us." He laughed. "Unless there is a Catholic marriage rite that allows a deacon to marry himself to someone. Somehow, I don't see that as much of a possibility. I doubt even any of the Protestants have that kind of ceremony in their prayerbook. How about the Lutherans, Eden? Are they that forward thinking?"

"Heavens no. But if Matty wants to *marry* us—as in perform the ceremony, I think it could be lovely. Then as soon as we're done with the wedding, he can quit. How fitting would that be? But Matty, how are we going to make you an irrevocable member of our union the way Nico's parents are? What will convince you if it's not marrying me legally instead of Nico? We need you to be one with us." She blushed. "I can barely believe I'm saying this, but there you have it. I love Nico so much, and I can see how deeply he loves you. Your connection is not something I want to disrupt. I feel certain that in time you and I can love one another that way as well. Take a chance on us, Matty. Please. Don't break Nico's heart all over again. His heart is too beautiful."

Matty let out a long breath and said, "You've given me a lot to think over."

THAT NIGHT OVER DINNER, THE ENTIRE FAMILY DISCUSSED possibilities for Matty's future. Isaac and Walter agreed that while looking for an amenable judge, they could also ask around for employment opportunities for a brilliant scholar. Walter's eyes sparkled when he said, "I have some very interesting ideas there, my boy."

Matty's heart lurched in his chest when he realized the kind of love this family was able to surround him with. It was sinking in that they weren't just being kind to the poor young man whose life was a mess right now; they truly loved him like their own and would do about anything for him. He wanted to be worthy of their love, but when he asked, "How can I ever repay you for everything you've done for me?" he was told that all they expected was for him to love Nico and Eden to the best of his ability and stop worrying so much.

"You'll find your way, Matty. You're a fine young man," Isaac told him.

Later that night, Eden and Nico surrounded him with a more carnal kind of love.

First, Nico decided it was time to educate Eden as to the finer points of oral pleasure. So he demonstrated on Matty, and when he had Matty moaning and jutting his hips, he stopped and told her to take over. Nico concentrated on Matty's backside while Eden began her experimentation. Instead of going at him tentatively, Eden gleefully embraced the actions she'd seen Nico use on Matty. She got him so worked up—especially when Nico bumped Matty's prostate with his long finger—Matty's chest was heaving when he cried out, "Ohh, that's perfect. Stop, or I won't last!"

When Matty once again slipped his rigid cock into Eden's paradise and heard her tender words, his heart began to warm. Nico again made love to Matty from behind at the same time, kissing his neck and promising him forever. "We'll make it work, Matty," he murmured. "Eden and I need you always."

Eden confirmed, "We do, Matty. Now, both of you, harder, please!" She squirmed and panted, coming apart as a climax raging like a stormy ocean crashed through her with wave after wave of ecstasy. She opened her eyes and stared straight into Matty's, whispering, "Let it go, dearest man. Fill me with your seed." That was all it took for Matty to erupt into her with Nico shaking and groaning behind him.

"That was incredible," Nico panted.

"It was," Matty agreed.

"Ohh. So good," Eden whispered. "We can do this—and more—for our whole lives, Matty. Just think of that."

PART

Three

THE YOUNG COUPLE LEFT FOR THE TRAIN STATION FIRST THING in the morning, driven by Isaac and Walter. Nico was excited, and Eden appeared nervous. Nico wasn't sure why, but she seemed reticent to talk about it, so he guessed it was because she'd felt so ill on the previous train ride. Suzette insisted that she take some snacks to nibble on as they traveled, so he hoped that would help.

Eden was actually worried to death about her parents' reaction to her arriving with Nico. She had a strong hunch that her father had already picked out a future husband for her. So she just had to hope showing up with a doctor for a son-in-law would impress them enough that her parents would accept their union. In any case, she hoped she could avoid letting them know about her pregnancy, but if she had to tell them, she would. There were so many ways this could go wrong, but

Nico had been adamant that he needed to ask for her hand properly before they married. *He has to pick this one thing to be traditional about.* She mentally shook her head.

As they traveled south, the scenery was fairly boring, but they did see some lovely orange groves and well-cared-for ranches. They debarked in Santa Ana, where Nico quickly found them transportation to the ranch, and they were off again. The weather was fine and the roads in decent shape, so the trip went as smoothly as it could. At least, for Nico.

Eden grew more silent and tense as they neared her home. Clouds of dust settled on their clothes and skin, so Nico wasn't all that eager to open his mouth to speak unnecessarily either. It was a relief to finally stop moving and climb down to the ground. He grabbed their bags, and the driver took off again immediately without so much as a goodbye. Nico offered his handkerchief to Eden so she could wipe her face off before doing so himself, and they headed to the door.

It wasn't locked, so Eden simply escorted Nico inside. Her family all sat around the dinner table having their evening meal. All conversation stopped, and multiple faces turned to look at them with startled expressions. Mrs. Godwin was the only female at the table among several men, so Nico assumed the various diners were both family and ranch hands.

"Well! Look who finally got here," Mr. Godwin announced in a rather unfriendly manner. "We expected you days ago."

Mrs. Godwin at least rose from the table, and Nico

expected her to embrace her daughter, but all she did was fetch a couple of plates and utensils. "You can sit here," she said, indicating the end of the table where there was still a bit of room. "There's chicken, beans, rolls, and potatoes." She looked at the young men sitting at the table and ordered, "Pass the serving dishes to Eden and her… guest."

"Thank you, ma'am," Nico said with a smile. "We need to wash up before eating."

"Suit yourselves. Eden can show you where." Looking at her sons and employees again, she added, "Leave some food for them, boys."

Eden stood up straight and cleared her throat. "Mama, Pa, I'd like to introduce you to Nicolo Stark-James. I wrote to you about him. He'd like to speak to you privately, Papa."

Her father snorted and answered under his breath, "We'll see about that."

A dark-haired fellow whom Nico guessed was their youngest son looked at Nico and asked, "What kind of name is that? You Italian or Spanish or something?"

Nico smiled and answered, "No. I'm half French and the other half is definitely American. I'm named for Nicolo Paganini, who was a violin instructor of my mother's when she was a young girl in France." Everyone screwed up their faces as if he'd spoken some foreign language. Clearly, music was not part of this family's repertoire. Nico was glad he hadn't added that Paganini was quite famous. He certainly didn't want them to think he was speaking down to them. He did add, however, "I'm pleased to meet all of you. Thank you for your hospitality, Mr. and Mrs. Godwin."

Mr. Godwin continued to eat, and Mrs. Godwin sat down looking tired and flustered.

Eden took Nico by the arm and pulled him out of the room.

When they reemerged looking cleaner and more refreshed, Nico noticed one of the men was gone, leaving an empty place with a half-eaten meal on the table.

"Where's Joshua, Mama?"

Before she could speak, Mr. Godwin answered for her. "I sent him out to check on… a birthing cow."

Her mother just looked at her plate and slowly shoveled food into her mouth.

Nico thought he heard the sound of horse hooves leaving the area, and that made him wonder where the cow was.

Conversation at the table went in fits and starts and focused mostly on how many of their avocado trees had died and how many calves had yet to be born. They nervously discussed plans for the next breeding cycle, ignoring Nico and Eden. Apparently, their best bull Solomon seemed rather sickly, and that worried all of them.

Nico was out of his element and therefore had nothing to contribute, so he tried asking a few general questions such as, "How long have you had this ranch?" and "How many head of cattle do you have, sir?"

Eden put her hand on his arm and shook her head slightly.

She whispered, "Never ask a rancher that. It's considered rude."

"Oh, sorry," he said to her father and then smiled charmingly—he hoped. "I'm a doctor, and I'm afraid I know nothing about the cattle business. Please don't take any offense. I'm sure having a ranch like this is quite fascinating. And you grow avocados too?"

Her father ignored him except for a loud snort. He looked at Eden finally, though, and asked, "Are you done with all of that stuff you wanted to do up north? You're not hoping to go back again in the fall, are you?"

Eden frowned and then answered proudly, "I'm finished with the program, and I'm a full-fledged nurse now."

"For whatever that's worth," her father answered.

"Her skills are impressive, sir, and nursing is a growing field with a lot of potential. I'm quite proud of her, and you should be as well," Nico said, beaming at Eden affectionately. "It's up to her as to how much or how little she ultimately wants to work in my Los Angeles clinic, but no matter what, I know she'll be a real asset."

Her father scooted back from the table, stood, and growled at Nico, "First of all, don't try to tell me what to think. And don't count on me agreeing with you if you do. Eden's place is right here. This is where she belongs. I figured a little medical knowledge might come in handy with the kind of hard labor we do around here, or I'd never have agreed to letting her go in the first place." He nodded to his wife and said, "I best be checking on that cow." He tossed his napkin into the middle of his plate and stomped toward the door.

Nico felt as if icy fingers gripped him by the scruff of his neck. *What?* He stood as well and asked, "Sir, may I have a word with you privately?" He figured he'd better ask for Eden's hand quickly. This visit was not going well, and they'd just arrived.

"No," was the older man's terse answer. He left the house, slamming the door behind him. One by one, the ranch hands followed him out the door, though less dramatically and with no acknowledgement to Mrs. Godwin for the meal. Her brothers silently shuffled up the stairs with their heads down.

Eden looked pale as she asked, "Mama? What's going on? Why is he so angry?"

Her mother wouldn't meet Eden's eyes as she answered, "That's for your pa to say."

"Yes, ma'am." Eden tried for a smile. "It's so nice to see you all finally. San Francisco was a wonderful adventure, but I missed you."

"Huh." Her mother got up and started to clear away the dishes. She paused as she gathered things and added, "You better do as your father tells you, or things won't go so well."

Nico couldn't help but compare this dinner to those in his house where lively, diverse conversation and laughter accompanied every meal. For some reason he couldn't fathom, the tension had been as thick as cold porridge at this table. And what her mother said sounded to his ears like a threat. His discomfort only increased when Mrs. Godwin added, "Show your guest out to the bunkhouse, Eden, and then come back and do the dishes. I have mending to do."

"Thank you for dinner, ma'am. I'll be happy to stay and help Eden do the dishes."

Mrs. Godwin gave Nico a steely glare and turned to walk away. Nico noticed how much—facial expressions aside—Eden looked like her mother, and it was then he realized her hands were red and chapped from heavy use, and she walked slowly as if she were bone tired. She shrugged and didn't answer his offer to help, so he assumed it would be acceptable.

It was completely dark outside when they finished the stack of dishes, and Eden explained, "I'd better take you out to the bunkhouse. You won't want to disturb any of the men who are likely asleep by now." She seemed disinclined to look Nico in the eye.

As they exited the front door, Nico asked quietly, "What's going on, Eden? Why is everyone so angry? Did we come at a bad time?"

"I'm not sure. My family isn't like yours, but it's not usually so grim around here, I promise." She finally looked up and tried for a smile. "I love you so much, Nico. Thank you for bringing me home, even if the reception hasn't been the most cordial. Maybe tomorrow I can show you around the ranch." They walked across a dusty area and stopped in front of a rough wooden door. "Here's the bunkhouse. I'm sorry if the accommodations aren't very comfortable. I thought they'd put you up in the spare room, but I guess I thought wrong. I can't go inside for obvious reasons, so you'll have to find your own bunk. There ought to be candles and matches by the door so you can find your way. The outhouse is out back. Again, I'm sorry. This is so different from your family's house."

"Nothing to be sorry about."

He wrapped his arms around her and was about to give her a kiss when the unmistakable sound of her father's voice boomed out, "Get yourself to bed, girl! And tell that young man not to disturb my hard-working men."

In the moonlight, Nico could see that her father's shirt was covered in blood. Nico's instant reaction was to ask, "Sir, are you hurt? Can I be of assistance?"

"Get to bed," was all he heard by way of a disgusted reply as Mr. Godwin stomped back to the house. But then the man mumbled something that sounded an awful lot like, "You'll be leaving soon enough, I hope."

"He's been delivering a calf," Eden explained. "Good night, Nico." She squeezed his hand and turned to follow her father back to the house.

Nico stood puzzling over them for a moment before opening the bunkhouse door and fumbling around in the dark for a candle. Once he managed to get one lit and into a holder, he tried to be as quiet as possible and not trip over anything. It took him a good ten minutes to discover there were no empty bunks anywhere, but there was a somewhat wide bench in the far corner that would have to do. It crossed his mind that

Eden's parents clearly had to know how many men there were and how many beds. Shaking his head, he removed his shoes and wadded up his shirt to use as a pillow. The air was pungent with the smells of livestock, manure, human sweat, and the ever-present dust. Several men were snoring and occasionally that sound would be punctuated by a loud fart. Nico was glad he'd skipped the beans at dinner. Thinking about dinner, he wondered if Eden knew how to cook any better than her mother. The food had been remarkably tasteless. He realized just how spoiled he'd been growing up with a skilled cook who took care of their meals. His own mother had often joked that she could barely boil water to make tea. This made him wonder if the Godwins' cook was on a vacation or they just didn't have one. But then he remembered Eden complaining about cooking endless meals and reminded himself that not everyone had grown up in a house with wealthy parents who could afford a household staff.

Sleeping on a hard wooden bench was also not something he was accustomed to, and it made him think about the stories his fathers told about the hardships they'd faced as they made their way across the country as part of a wagon train to California and how they'd nearly frozen to death crossing the Sierra Nevada. He knew he was fortunate and had no call to complain over a hard place to sleep for one night when his parents had sacrificed so much to make a great life for him and his siblings. Still… he was darned uncomfortable and confused by Eden's parents and their uncordial attitude toward him. Something was clearly up with that. He fretted and stewed about it until sheer exhaustion finally took over and he fell asleep.

His rest did not last long enough for him, even though the other bunkhouse occupants were gone by the time Nico's sleep was shattered. He was rudely awakened by a rough hand covering his mouth like a lead weight and strong arms dragging him upright. At first, Nico was too shocked to struggle, but then sheer terror filled him, and he began to twist around violently as he chomped down on the hand covering his mouth.

"Ow! The son of a bitch bit me!" This came from Eden's brother Joshua who'd left dinner supposedly to take care of a cow. He pulled his hand back and shook it.

"Quiet, you big baby!" grumbled the man with a vise grip on Nico.

"Let go of me!" Nico hollered. "Help!"

"Shut up, or you'll be sorry." The hands tightened their grip. "I have a gun."

Nico continued to struggle until someone clobbered him in the face, making him see stars. The shock of the blow momentarily made Nico stop thrashing.

Joshua began grumbling even more about his hand and then said, "Listen, you ornery shit. You're going to leave my sister alone, hear me? She's spoken for, and she's gonna marry the love of her life here, Silas Hatchett."

"She is *not*," Nico argued with conviction. He hoped his

teeth were all still intact and ran his tongue around exploringly. He could taste blood, but nothing seemed to be missing or loose. *Thank heaven.*

"I don't know what she's been telling you, but we've been in love for a quite a while," Silas explained in an oily voice. "I was just waiting for her to finish that nonsense up north and come home so we could unite in holy matrimony at last. Thanks for delivering her. You saved me the trip."

"If she's so in love with you, why didn't she ever mention your name to me? And why does she hate it here so much? Are *you* the reason?" It would certainly make sense, Nico thought to himself.

"Look, boy, we're going to get you off this ranch, and if you don't start cooperating, I'm gonna drag you off behind the wagon, and I hear tell that getting dragged ain't no picnic," Silas said with a sneer. "Might be fun for me, though."

"I'm not leaving here without Eden!"

"Stick something in this fool's mouth before he wakes up the dead, Josh."

Joshua left for a moment while Nico continued to holler for help and thrash around, trying to extricate himself from Silas' grip. Although similar in size to Nico, Silas had years of backbreaking labor on his side, and he was as strong as an ox.

When Joshua returned with a smelly sock, Nico clamped his mouth shut as firmly as a bank vault. When Joshua tried to pry his mouth open, Nico bit him again and turned his face away quickly, spitting out the disgusting edge of the sock while Joshua shook his hand. "Damned city boy!"

Joshua was so angry, he made a fist with his unscathed hand and plowed it into Nico's gut. Fortunately, Nico saw it coming and tensed up his muscles, but it still took the wind out of him and hurt like the devil. He gagged and tried to suck in a breath while Silas held Nico's hands behind his back and wrapped a cord around them, tying them securely. Then Joshua took the filthy sock and crammed it into Nico's gaping mouth, and Silas tied it in place with a rope.

Silas tried to haul Nico to his feet roughly, which was no easy task because Nico, having no desire to get up, acted like dead weight and didn't help him a bit. Joshua approached closer to help Silas, so Nico kicked out with his stockinged foot and caught Joshua right in the balls. This made him double over and gag.

"Quit messing around, Josh. Get up and help me get this pile of dung outta here!"

Joshua merely made retching noises loudly punctuated by Nico's muffled hollering. Silas let go with one hand long enough to grab one of Nico's shoes and smash him in the temple with it. Nico's last conscious thought was, *I hope I don't end up with brain damage*. He swayed and passed out.

Over the next however long it was—Nico had no idea—he became vaguely aware of nearly smothering under a heavy tarp that smelled like shit and a hard, jostling surface beneath him. He was lying on top of his hands, which was extremely uncomfortable. The sound of hooves, rattling of wheels, and the buzzing of flies were the only noises he could detect. He also gradually became aware that his feet were tied like his hands. He wouldn't be delivering anymore kicks to anyone's soft, lumpy spots, that was certain. The heat that bore down on him made him think that the sun had risen, so he'd been moving for a while. He wiggled his hands and toes experimentally, grateful at least that his circulation wasn't impaired. That was about the only positive thing he could come up with, but then he cheered up more when he realized he was also alive and apparently not addle-brained from the blow to his head. To test himself, he went through the names of bones in the body according to groups. He was heartened to realize that he was fine. His head ached and he was terribly thirsty, but apart from that, his body appeared unscathed—at least as far as any permanent damage went.

After a while, the conveyance stopped, and he could hear muffled voices. He detected a sound that might be a barn door opening, and the jostling started up again for just a moment. He felt like they'd moved inside a barn because the heat of the sun on his cover seemed to decrease. He could hear the sounds of two horses being unhitched from what he assumed was the wagon that carried him, and it sounded as if they were led to stalls. Finally, the filth-encrusted tarp was torn away from him in a cloud of dust that made his eyes water. They were indeed inside a rather spacious barn.

Silas and Joshua dragged Nico from the back of the

wagon, earning him a few painful splinters in his hands along the way. They set him on his feet, and Silas explained to him, "Look mister. I don't particularly want to kill you on account I'd have that on my conscience for a while if I did. However, I will if I have to. And you'll end up somewhere no one will find you. So I'm going to tie you up over here to this post, and Josh is going to undo your gag…"

"Why me?" Joshua protested. "He'll just bite me again!"

Ignoring him, Silas continued. "You probably need water, so I'm going to be a nice fellow and give you some. But pay me some mind here. There is no one around for miles, so you can yell and scream your head off and all you're going to accomplish is getting yourself a sore throat. Don't even bother. It'll just make me mad, and you don't want that." He dragged Nico over to a wooden beam and tied him to it, then he looked sharply at Joshua and ordered, "Get on with it! We don't have all day."

Joshua gingerly plucked at the binding that held the sock in Nico's mouth, and once he had it untied, he snagged the edge of the material quickly as though he were trying to avoid the fangs of a rabid dog. As soon as he finished, Silas ordered him, "Now take your horse and skedaddle on home, Josh. You don't want to be involved in case I do have to kill this fool here. And keep your trap shut when you get to your pa's place."

Nico's mouth was so dry, he coughed and had the strongest urge to spit out the flavor of stinky foot from his mouth, but he couldn't produce any saliva. Within a few moments, however, Silas produced a small cup of water that he generously held up to Nico's mouth. Nico drank greedily but did not offer his thanks. He simply glared at Silas, wondering how many horrible things he was swallowing with the water. Once the cup was empty, Silas pulled up a crate and sat in front of Nico with a serious expression on his face.

"Now, I need to tell you something," Silas began. "I'm not a bad man." Nico scoffed, but Silas ignored him. "All of this is because I'm helping out Eden's family and doing something her father has wanted—and needed—for years. You see, his ranch is not the most successful around here. He's had a heap of trouble with his water supply. He's been trying to get me to partner with him and combine our ranches. He has more acreage and had more livestock until he couldn't keep them healthy anymore, but I have better land. So we cut a deal after my wife passed and my sons lit outta here. He'd give me Eden, and we'd all become one big, happy family. Eden hasn't been too cooperative, so we agreed to let her go off and try doing something on her own for a while, certain she'd hate it. I know for a fact that she hates the sight of blood, so becoming a nurse sounded pretty hare-brained to me. But… she insisted, and I'm an open-minded man. I'm reasonably patient, but I've waited long enough.

"Then her family's ranch began having some *serious* trouble about the same time that Eden started writing those sappy letters home to her parents saying she was in love. Well, mister, we can't have that. She's supposed to love me! She's *my* future wife. So if you care about her and her family, you'll understand that her daddy's ranch ain't going to last much longer without my help. I've watched that girl grow up from a spindly legged brat to a beautiful woman, and you barely know her. She's mine, and that's all there is to it. What we're going to do is you're going to write her a letter telling her that you've changed your mind and you've headed for home. You do that, and I'll send you up to the train myself. Don't do it, and… well, we have some hungry damned buzzards out in the desert to the east of here."

Nico briefly considered telling Silas that Eden was pregnant, and he was the proud father, but the man seemed a bit unhinged and definitely dangerous. The convenient passing of Silas's wife and disappearance of his sons when Eden became of marriageable age troubled Nico, so he decided silence was the best route to take. Faking acquiescence seemed even more prudent, even though he had absolutely no intention of leaving Eden in this man's clutches. "Fair enough," he answered hoarsely. He'd figure out something to do. "I'll write her a letter. You'll just have to untie my hands." Then he added rather piteously, "Just please don't hurt me." He hoped Silas would think he was simple-minded, or at the very least, cowardly.

"You bet, sonny. I'll go fetch something to write with. You wait here." He cackled at his own joke and sauntered away. Before he left the barn, Silas drew his pistol and gave it a quick, showy spin on his finger before re-holstering it. Nico recognized that for the warning it clearly was.

Left with nothing to do, Nico gazed around the spacious barn that housed several horses. Nico noticed it was quite clean and smelled better than the Godwins' bunkhouse had— probably due to the lack of people in the barn. There was the smell of horses, of course, but also alfalfa, fresh straw bedding, and clean tack. Silas Hatchett may be a little crazy, but he kept things tidy, although the structure itself looked like it needed some serious repairs. He wondered where the ranch hands were, or if there were any at all. Nico suddenly realized he needed to stop woolgathering and come up with a plan to let Eden know he was *not* deserting her.

He had plenty of time to think, as it turned out—it took Silas an awful long time to return. Nico noticed a mild aroma of coffee and bacon about the man when he reappeared; he'd obviously stopped inside for some breakfast. Nico ignored his own rumbling stomach.

True to his word, Silas produced a pencil and paper and undid Nico's right hand, then scooted the crate over so Nico would have a flat surface to write on, but he had to bend awkwardly to get to it, and it was hard to stay upright with his feet lashed together. Seeing the problem, Silas brought another crate over so Nico could sit down to write at least. Nico didn't bother to thank him for his thoughtfulness.

His mind raced with possibilities. It was imperative that she know he was being held against his wishes and had no desire to leave her. Considering Eden's previous unwillingness to go along with her family's arranged marriage plans, Nico hoped she would be on the lookout for clues in his letter.

Silas was looking impatient and fiddling with his gun, so Nico put the pencil to the paper as Silas spun his pistol around.

Eden,

Now that I have seen where you come from, I think we are too different for this marriage to work. I'm leaving this morning to return to my family home in San Francisco and won't be seeing you again. I'm sure you'll be happy with Hatchett on his ranch. He seems like a thoughtful man, and it's the best place for you. Wishing you a healthy life.

Nicolo Matthew James-Stark

NICO WAS PRETTY CERTAIN EDEN WOULD SEE THROUGH ALL OF his falsehoods enough to be warned, and he thought the letter looked innocent enough not to alert Silas of its deception. It was all he could do at the moment. He hoped no one remembered his last name from Eden's introduction, but he thought it unlikely that anyone was paying close enough attention and would remember it was actually Stark-James. He also hoped lying about San Francisco and invoking Matty's name would strike a chord.

Silas saw that Nico was done and snatched the paper from him. He read it quickly, folded it in half, and stuffed it in his pocket. "I might let you live after all," he growled at Nico as he yanked him into a standing position and re-tied his hand to the post. He viciously kicked the crates out of Nico's reach. Then he added a rope around Nico's neck for good measure, securing it to a side support. "Now you need to just sit tight here while I go take care of some business, and I'll be back for you later." Cackling like a maniac, he repeated, "Sit tight," like it was the funniest joke on earth. Smirking, he spun his pistol around another couple of times before exiting the barn on a handsome chestnut horse.

Nico had a lot of thinking to do.

WHILE ALL OF THIS WAS GOING ON WITH NICO, BACK AT THE Godwin ranch, Eden had roused herself from bed and descended the stairs to find her mother busily preparing a mountain of food for the next meal. "Where's Nico, Mama?" she asked with a yawn.

Without looking up or pausing what she was doing, Mrs. Godwin answered in a bored tone, "He must be as lazy as you. I haven't seen him."

"Sorry, Mama, I couldn't help sleeping in. I was exhausted. But didn't he come in for breakfast?"

"I told you I haven't seen him. Either he's still sleeping, or he lit out of here."

Frowning, Eden muttered to herself, "That's strange. I'm sure he'd be hungry by now, and he wouldn't have left." She headed outside for the bunkhouse. Stopping at the door, she knocked loudly and called, "Nico, are you up? Come on in the house and get something to eat."

When there was no response, she tried knocking again and hollering, "Nico? Come on out!"

That summons also got no response, so she figured none of the workers must be inside. She opened the door and stuck her head in. "Phew! These men need to do some laundry. It smells awful in here," she grumbled. Looking around the dim interior, she could see there was no one there. The place was such a mess—she didn't spot Nico's shoes on the floor, but it was obvious that the man himself was missing. She quickly withdrew from the doorway and headed back to the house.

"Mama, he's not out there. Someone must know where he is."

"Well, I am not that someone. Now eat something so you can help me. Hurry up."

"But Nico is *missing*! I need to find him."

"He's a grown man who doesn't need you traipsing around looking for him. He's probably halfway back to Los Angeles by now if he has any sense. So forget about him and get busy. I'm tired of this whining."

With her stomach churning, Eden realized she absolutely needed to eat something before she could figure out what was going on, so she grabbed a bowl and dished up a serving of porridge from the stove. It tasted like mud, but at least it would help settle her stomach.

While she ate her breakfast, there was a knock at the door.

"Get that, will you, Eden?"

"Yes, ma'am."

The man at the door was a stranger. He smiled and handed her a piece of paper.

Eden took one quick look at the contents of the note and had to sit down before her legs gave out.

Eighteen

ON HIS WAY BACK TO THE GODWIN RANCH, JOSHUA DECIDED to take the route he and his brothers used when they were little and liked to play along the creek—even if it would take him a little longer to get home. He didn't much care for the idea of anyone seeing him leave the Hatchett ranch and preferred to avoid the road. As much as he pretended to pay attention to Silas and do his bidding when his father ordered him to, the man gave him the creeps. Joshua was *not* looking forward to being his brother-in-law.

He was riding along, not really paying attention, when his horse stepped into some difficult footing and made squishy, splashing noises. Looking down, he noticed that where it used to be pastureland for grazing, it now looked more like a rice paddy. The land was flooded!

"How can this be?" he wondered aloud. "*Our* ranch is dry

as a bone!" They were having lots of trouble with the lack of water and assumed it was because of the dry season and poor run-off. Curious, he prowled around the perimeter of this new swampy area he'd never seen before and finally found its cause.

"That dirty, rotten sidewinder Silas Hatchett!" he spat out. "He's gone and built a dam and cut off most of our water supply!" He could see that where there used to be a rushing stream, there was now a weak trickle heading to his family's ranch. Quickly, he reined his horse around and headed for drier terrain. He'd have to use the road after all or risk getting his horse stuck in the soggy land. He was carefully picking his way through a thicket of trees when he saw none other than Silas Hatchett himself barreling along on his sweaty horse, spurring the animal viciously as they galloped by.

Joshua was fairly certain he hadn't been spotted. He hoped. He wasn't sure where Silas was headed, but he prayed it wasn't their ranch. He had to get home and tell his pa what was going on. He peeked out from behind a massive boulder, waiting until he couldn't see Silas and his horse anymore. Then he was torn. Should he go back and get Eden's friend or continue on and tell his pa?

"Oh, hell," he muttered. "I hate that man almost as much for biting me as I hate Silas, so he can get his own self outta trouble." He headed for home at a brisk pace.

He was nearly back to the family ranch when he spied Silas again. He pulled up sharply on his horse's reins and moved off the road, observing Silas. He was standing next to his horse talking to a man Joshua didn't recognize. He could see something small change hands, and then the stranger held out his hand with an impatient "gimme" attitude. Silas dropped some coins into the man's hand.

"Oh no!" Joshua whispered to himself. Silas had remounted his horse and was now heading back in his direction. There was absolutely nowhere to hide. He'd have to think fast. Instead of turning around and running, Joshua proceeded toward Silas in a leisurely fashion and tried to adopt a carefree attitude. He grinned at Silas and called out, "Fancy seeing you again this morning so soon."

Silas narrowed his eyes and glared at Joshua, asking, "Why didn't I pass you? Where have you been?"

"Oh, you did pass me, and I must say, ol' Rusty there's a fast one!"

"I didn't pass you. I'd have seen you."

Joshua tried to laugh and make it sound authentic. "I'm glad you didn't see me—it woulda been embarrassing. I had to dismount and take care of my morning constitutional, if you know what I mean. I was so miserable I couldn't ride another step until I emptied myself, so I found a grove of trees over yonder." He waved his hand in a vague manner in the opposite direction of the dammed-up stream. "Taking care of business took a lot longer than I expected. See, I wasn't feeling so good actually. But now I'm fine, and I'll be home in a couple a minutes. So, I guess I'll be seeing you later." He gave his horse a good nudge in the ribs and took off at a lope. He didn't want to stick around any longer to see what Silas might have to say. Fortunately, he was close to home. As soon as he arrived, he saw the man Silas had paid handing a piece of paper over to Eden at the door. The stranger tipped his hat and kept walking away from the ranch. Mrs. Godwin called him back and handed him half a loaf of bread. The man spoke to her with a smile and a nod and left once more.

Not wanting to waste another moment, Joshua headed toward the bunkhouse and saw one of the hands on his way out pulling on a pair of gloves. "I need to speak to my parents right away. It's an emergency. Can you take care of my horse?" he asked the man.

"Oh, well, sure. I forgot my gloves, but I was just going to meet up with your father. He's in the barn. I'll let him know you need him."

"Thanks!" Joshua jogged off toward the house.

Inside, he found his sister sitting red-eyed and confused, staring at a piece of paper. She looked up quickly and glared at her brother. "I hope you have nothing to do with this, Josh!"

"I don't know what you have there, but as soon as Pa comes in, I have to tell all of you something bad." He saw his sister go as pale as a sheet and added, "Your friend was still kicking when I saw him last, so I don't think Silas has hurt him—well, not yet anyway."

"Something is very, very wrong!" Eden hollered at him. "Nico sent me a nonsensical note saying he's leaving, and he thinks I'll be happy with that horrible old man! He *knows* better!"

Her father stomped into the house just as she complained about Silas, and he glared at her. "You shut your mouth, Eden!" he shouted. "That man may be the only way we can keep this ranch going, and you owe it to us to help in the way we agreed!"

"*You* agreed! No one considered asking me!"

"*Shut up, both of you*!" Joshua screamed at them. "Listen to me! This is an emergency!"

His mother, father, and sister were dumbfounded by his outburst and stared at him with wide eyes. Joshua was not known for being outspoken; he was always the one who took orders without question.

"Silas tricked us, Pa. I just saw that he dammed up the creek. That part of his land is nearly flooded, and the stream is barely trickling through to our land. We don't have a water problem at all. We have a Silas Hatchett problem! This was just another way to guarantee he'd get Eden. He was probably planning to cut off the water completely and starve us out so he could buy the property for nothing. Then he'd have Eden *and* our ranch. On top of that, he kidnapped Nick… Nicko… or whatever his name is, and he's got him tied up in his barn, and I think he means to kill him. I hope to hell that isn't gonna happen even if he did bite me."

Eden screwed up her face. "Nico *bit* you?"

"Well, yeah. Let's just say, he probably felt he had a reason for it, and I'm sorry, Sis. I never shoulda helped Silas. I truly thought it was the only way to save the ranch." He looked at his pa. "We have to get Nico away from that crook. I don't like the rumors about how his wife died suddenly, and I don't trust Hatchett. At. All."

"We need the sheriff," Mrs. Godwin said. "Right away."

"I still have calves to deliver!" Mr. Godwin bellowed.

Bellowing right back at him, his wife argued, "You're not going to have a ranch left at all if you let that man continue to take advantage of you, so let the hands take care of the calves, and go fetch the sheriff! You can't let Silas hurt Nico."

"I'll go get the sheriff, and you go find Nico and get him away from Silas!" Eden demanded. "Go now! If so much as one hair on that man's head is harmed, I'll hold you responsible for the rest of your lives. I love him and he's the *father of my baby*!" With an instinctive protectiveness, she hugged her belly.

Mr. Godwin's face turned a nasty shade of purple and he raised his hand at Eden, but his wife grabbed his arm and cried out, "Don't you even dare!" Glaring at him she added, "What would you have done if my pa had hit me for loving you? Think about that!"

Godwin had the grace to look at least a little chastised, and he lowered his hand. "I thought we raised you better than that, girl," he added anyway. His wife scoffed at him, and Eden glowered.

"I will love and marry whomever I please! And it sure

isn't going to be Silas Hatchett," she nearly shouted. "I am not your property to sell like livestock!" Her chest heaved with emotion as she glared at her father. "Now I'm going to go grab one of the horses and fetch the sheriff to take him back to Hatchett's ranch. I expect to see you and my brothers there when I get back. Nico does not deserve to pay for the mistake you made of putting your trust in that horrible man, so do your duty and try to make sure he's not harmed. Go *now*!"

"She makes a good point, Abner," Mrs. Godwin said to her husband. "It's not Nico's fault, and he's caught up in a dangerous situation."

"Stop wasting time! I'm leaving," Eden cried. She rushed out the door toward the barn.

"Damned Silas!" Abner grumbled. "He was just supposed to get Nico off the ranch, not hurt him!"

"You better take your pistol," Mrs. Godwin said.

Nico felt dreadful. He hoped like crazy that Eden had received the note and she'd seen through his ruse. He also hoped Silas wasn't going to return and shoot him—or feed him to the buzzards—or both. His head ached, he hurt all over, and smelled to high heaven—plus he was hungry, thirsty, and desperately needed to pee. *How on earth did everything wind up going so poorly? Just two days ago, I was planning a life with Eden and hopefully Matty, and now I'm not sure I'll live to see tomorrow. One thing is certain, I don't want to sit here like a captured rabbit and wait for that maniac to come back here and feed me to the desert scavengers.*

The first order of business was that he needed to get himself free from these ropes. His hands were fastened to the wooden post, so that seemed like the logical place to begin. He pulled against the bonds, but they stayed tight. "Damned cattleman. He knows how to tie a rope," he muttered. The next possibility might be the sturdiness of the beam itself. It looked somewhat rotten—as if maybe termites had invaded the wood. He wondered if the roof might cave in if he managed to knock it down. But there were other roof supports, so the horses in the barn ought to be safe enough. He began to knock against it with his shoulder. After a few agonizing minutes of that, the wood developed a decent crack. After a few more minutes, it splintered in two, and Nico raised up his hands and slid the rope off. He was still tied, but not tied to anything. Unfortunately, the part of the wood his neck was tied to went the wrong direction and pulled against him, nearly cutting off his air supply.

Now he could free his hands, but he was still stuck. He couldn't bend over to untie his feet because he'd choke to death, and he couldn't do anything to the rope around his neck except make it tighter. "What a pickle," he grunted. The only problem he could do anything about was relieving his bursting bladder. So Nico undid his trousers and let fly with a gallon or so of urine—spraying it as far away from his feet as possible since he had no shoes. He had just finished tucking himself back in when Silas came trotting into the barn with his exhausted, sweaty horse whose sides were heaving. He'd obviously run the horse too hard and for too long.

Looking at the state of his barn and the rotten beam, Silas glared at Nico and shouted, "You've ruined my property! Now you're gonna have to pay for that."

Nico was afraid to say anything because he could barely get enough air to breathe and definitely not enough to have a debate with an insane person. He kept his hands close to where he'd been tied, hoping Silas wouldn't see that they were actually free from the wooden beam.

Ignoring Nico for the time being, Silas unsaddled his horse. Nico thought it was awful for the man to turn the horse into a stall without letting the horse cool down first. The animal needed to be walked around for a while to let his breathing go back to normal or he might end up sick. Just another thing about Silas Hatchett to hate.

Silas put away the tack and then approached Nico, pulling his gun out of his holster. With an evil grin, he started to flip his gun around with one of his twirly finger spins when… *pow*!

The gun went off.

CHAPTER

Twenty

Joshua, his brothers, and his father were approaching Silas' property—though they were still a ways off from the barn—when they heard the unmistakable report of a gun. They looked at each other in alarm and sped up.

"Please be alive, Nico," Joshua pled in a whisper. "My sister will kill me if you aren't."

As they neared the barn, they dismounted and left their horses in the shade of a tree. Abner Godwin drew his gun, and they approached the barn door stealthily. All was as quiet as a tomb. But then, they heard a scratchy voice pleading, "Help!"

They peered around the edge of the open door and saw the strangest sight ever. Nico was trussed up with a rope around his neck like someone had tried to hang him from a rotten timber, and his feet were lashed together. He was clearly on the verge of choking to death because the timber was starting to give, and it was falling away from him, taking his air supply with it.

And a few feet away lay Silas Hatchett, having bled to death from a big hole in his neck and his pistol still firmly in his hand.

Clearly, Silas was beyond help, so Joshua ran in search of a knife or a saw to cut Nico down before he expired, and Abner rushed to raise Nico's body up to alleviate some of the pressure on his throat. Within minutes, they had him cut loose, and Nico sucked in massive amounts of air.

"We owe you a huge apology, son," Abner said to him when Nico started to look normal again. "Are you fit to talk to the sheriff? Eden went to fetch him, and hopefully they ought to be here soon."

"The dirty bastard was cheating us!" Joshua explained. "I can't say I'm sorry he's gone."

"I'll be fine," Nico said in a relieved voice and looked at Joshua. "You'll want to clean up that hand of yours and keep it clean."

"Eh, I guess I had it coming, what with the sock and all."

"I guess you probably did. How's Eden? Does she hate me for leaving?"

"No, son. Josh explained that you'd been taken against your will, and she explained that she loves you. I realize now that forcing her to marry Silas was a huge mistake. I wish you'd waited a little longer—like *after* the wedding—to get her in a family way, but I understand. It happens."

"She told you?"

"Yeah."

"So do I have your blessing to marry her?"

"I can't say no."

"Thank you, sir. This sure isn't the way I'd expected to ask though—standing next to a dead body."

"Did he commit suicide?" Joshua asked. "Right in front of you?"

"No. He was showing off to intimidate me and spinning his gun around on his finger when he slipped in the puddle of piss I made. He fell, and the gun went off. Damned stupid of him."

Joshua spent the next several minutes explaining exactly what he'd discovered on the property to Nico and his father when Eden and the sheriff came bursting through the door. Eden took one look at Silas and ran back outside again and retched into the grass.

Nico ran after her and waited for her to straighten up. He drew her into his arms and told her, "I was so afraid I'd never see you again. He wanted to kill me."

"I'm so sorry I brought you here, Nico. Will you ever forgive me?"

"Eden, I wanted to come here. None of this was your fault. I love you as much as ever. Never doubt that. I just want to get cleaned up and go home. Your father gave us his blessing, by the way."

Mr. Godwin came out to get Nico, saying, "The sheriff

needs to hear exactly what happened. We told him what we saw, so he knows you were tied up and had nothing to do with the shooting, but he'd like to hear it all from you as well."

"I can't go back in there, so I'll go sit with the horses," Eden said with a shiver. "Too much blood."

Just then, one of her brothers came running out of the barn holding a sack. "Lookit what I found in his feed room, Pa. Poison! He could've had rats, or… this might be what's been ailing ol' Solomon the bull. Maybe Silas was slipping it into his feed somehow."

Abner Godwin scowled and answered, "It's definitely a possibility. We'll see if that poor bull's health improves now that Silas isn't sneaking around to mess with him."

NICO AND EDEN WANTED TO GET BACK TO LOS ANGELES IN the worst way, but Nico decided it might be a good idea to stick around a little longer and help Eden's family repair the dammed-up water flow into their land. Even with postponing the branding, they had more to do than they could handle, but the water situation took precedence. It was backbreaking work, but he told her, "They've had to put up with a lot of trouble lately, and another set of hands should be welcome." So he borrowed some work clothes and got busy.

"I love you all the more for this, Nico," she told him. "Most men would turn their back on my family for what they almost did."

"They've been under a lot of stress lately. No one is at their best under those circumstances. One thing Matty has taught me by example is the importance of showing grace in the face of adversity. I'd rather stay and help make your family's lives better than run away because they made me angry. Unfortunately for both of us, the situation got to be awfully dangerous. But it was Hatchett—not your family."

As a form of apology, the Godwin family moved Nico out of the bunkhouse and into their spare room with a real bed. He spent three nights that way with Eden sneaking into his room each evening and out in the wee hours of the morning.

They were extra quiet but terribly happy to be together.

As expected, Solomon the bull began to take more of an interest in eating and strutting around like the big Casanova he was. The upcoming breeding season was looking better and better.

"I wonder how many other downstream spreads were affected by that horrible man's selfishness with the water," Mrs. Godwin mused over the meal preparations with Eden. "I can't believe he was actually flooding his own land."

On the day Eden and Nico planned to leave, there was a knock at the door while they were all having breakfast. Joshua rose to open the door. Surprised, he stepped back and said, "Come on in!"

It was two of Silas Hatchett's three sons who'd come to apologize for what their father had done. Apparently, word traveled quickly. After accepting their condolences over the loss of their father with a polite nod, the elder son explained, "Our other brother moved to Idaho with his new wife, and we took jobs in Santa Ana when we realized we couldn't work with our pa any longer. We had to come back for a while, though, to take care of the livestock. Thank you for feeding the horses until we could get here. The thing is, we're not interested in ranching anymore, and we wondered if you'd like to buy the property and the animals and increase your ranch that way. We'll sell it all to you cheap. It just holds bad memories for us."

Abner looked surprised and then sorry when he answered, "I'd love to do that, but lately we've been hanging on by a thread, so we don't have the cash to pay you. I'm sorry. It was good of you to come to us first though."

Nico spoke up, "Sir, I might be able to help." Everyone's attention snapped to him. "My family is always looking for investments. If you wanted some silent partners, perhaps they'd be interested. I can certainly speak to them and let you know as soon as Eden and I get back to Los Angeles."

Abner looked pleasantly surprised and said to the Hatchetts, "If you don't mind waiting a few more days, we'll see what Nico's family has to say. He's about to become my son-in-law. In the meantime, we'll keep helping you with the livestock. That's a lot for the two of you to handle by yourselves." Turning to Nico, he said with a smile, "Thank you, son." Then turning to Eden, he said, "He's one in a million. Treat this young man well."

"I plan to, Pa." She grinned happily at Nico.

Twenty~Two

With the situation resolved on the ranch, Eden and Nico turned their attention back to their upcoming wedding. They discussed their various options on the way home.

As expected, Eden's parents had wished them well and said they would not be able to take the time to travel up to Los Angeles for the wedding.

On the train, Eden told Nico, "It makes me sad they can't come, but it's also rather a relief to know we won't have to explain too much to them about Matty. That is, if Matty agrees to be a part of our union. You know I'm not in love with him yet, but if you love him as much as you do, I think it will happen quickly for me too." She was glad they had a private compartment so they could speak freely. Her stomach was far more settled on this train journey than it had been on the way south, perhaps because she wasn't so nervous.

"I understand your feelings completely," Nico answered. "We'll still have to work on him to agree to be with us, no doubt." He looked at her with love in his eyes and said, "I am so happy that you are accepting of this. It takes a special woman to take on two men at once and love us both. I was afraid we might scare you off."

Eden laughed softly. "Most women don't understand what they're missing. I feel like the luckiest woman in the world."

"I hope we can make sure you always feel that way. I know I'm the luckiest man."

It was late evening by the time they made it back to the Stark-James estate, and everyone there was relaxing in the study after dinner. Walter was reading, Matty and Isaac were playing chess, and Suzette was practicing the Bach/Gounod Ave Maria on her violin. It was such a peaceful, domestic scene, Eden hated to break it up. They all stopped what they were doing as soon as the couple entered the room, and Eden exclaimed, "I'm sorry we disturbed you! Please go on with your music."

Suzette laughed and set down her instrument, rushing to kiss them both and welcome them home. "Nonsense," she told Eden. "We are thrilled to have you both back again finally, and besides, that music sounds much better with Adeline accompanying me on the piano. Why have you been gone for so long?"

"We have plenty to tell you," Nico answered, squeezing Eden's hand.

After lots of hugs and kisses—especially with Matty—they all trooped back into the dining room where food was brought out for the tired travelers. Suzette took a long look at her son and asked, "Nicolo, dear, why are you so sunburned, and what happened to your neck? It looks like a rope burn!"

"Yes, well…" Nico and Eden's story unfolded in bits and pieces while Nico's parents and Matty sipped glasses of brandy. They alternated between disbelief, horror, relief, and delight as the adventure played out in the retelling.

Nico discovered he was famished and made a promise to himself to go thank the cook for a wonderful meal as soon as he was done eating. He'd had no idea how great she was before sampling ranch food made by a terribly overworked woman.

"And I received Mr. Godwin's blessing after all," Nico announced after they'd heard the entire harrowing tale. "He even knows that Eden is expecting, and her mother gave us a beautiful, knitted blanket she used for her babies. She said she kept it to give to their first grandchild."

"How are you feeling, Eden?" Suzette asked.

"Very well, thank you. I'm tired but extremely happy."

Matty had been somewhat quiet while Nico and Eden ate, delighting in just looking fondly at both of them, happy to have them back. When their story was finished, however, he smiled broadly and announced, "That was quite an experience the two of you had. Now I have something important to share with you."

PART

Four

CHAPTER

Twenty~Three

PICKING UP IMMEDIATELY ON MATTY'S MOOD, NICO ASKED excitedly, "What is it?"

"I haven't told any of you yet because I wanted to wait until Eden and Nico were back."

This captured everyone's undivided attention.

"I kept feeling as if I needed a mentor, but we all know Father Andrew has ulterior motives and has outlived his usefulness for me because of that. I needed someone who was more removed from my life who could see things clearly. So, yesterday I went back to our old school to visit with Father Kiefer."

"Our old Latin teacher!" exclaimed Nico with a big grin. "I know you enjoyed that class and all of the Roman history he taught us along with the Latin. He was wonderful."

"He still is wonderful, but his eyesight is failing, and he's ready to retire from teaching. We had a long conversation, and I won't go into all of it, but he thinks I ought to take over his classes."

"Matty, that would be perfect!" Nico cried. "So much better for you than becoming a priest." Then he sobered as his hopes took a tumble. "They don't expect you to take vows, do they?" As far as he could remember, all of their instructors had been priests.

Matty chuckled. "No, but he was glad I'd been to seminary and said because of that, they might even have me teach more than just Latin—I'm hoping he meant religious history or philosophy—but being a deacon was fine with them, and if I prefer to become a lay teacher, that will also work. Things are changing a bit in the school to keep up with the times." He grinned. "Anyway, I spoke to the headmaster who remembered me as well, and the two of them together acted like I'd shown up bearing gifts. They weren't at all sure of what they were going to do for a new teacher and said I was an answer to their prayers. The fact that I'd been a student there weighed heavily in my favor, even though I ended up somewhere else. They knew all about the school I went to and said it was also well-respected." Looking very pleased with himself, he added, "They assumed I knew that the boarding school was tuition-free because it was designed for students who are in unusual situations—some are orphans, and some had problems at their previous school—but still needed a good Catholic education. So now I know that's one less debt I owe anyone. No thanks to Father Andrew for letting me in on *that* information."

"What about Father Andrew?" Nico asked. "Have you spoken to him about this?"

"I haven't been able to speak to him about anything yet. He's clearly been avoiding me. I'm not sure what he's trying to accomplish."

"How strange," Walter said thoughtfully. Everyone agreed with him; it was odd behavior.

They also concurred that Matty's conversation with Father Kiefer was potentially marvelous, and Suzette said Matty's news called for a celebration. Matty demurred, however, and cautioned them, "Let's see if I can extricate myself from Father Andrew's demands first and get a contract with the school before we have a party. You never know. Maybe the school board will somehow find me unacceptable. Maybe some of them knew my father, and they won't take kindly to a failed priest who's the son of a bankrupt alcoholic teaching the young men of Los Angeles. Let's remain cautiously optimistic. Besides, there is a wedding to plan, and that's far more important than where I work."

"Nonsense, Matty. You're as important to us as we are to each other. Whatever affects you is going to affect us for the rest of our lives. Remember that." He looked at Eden, who was stifling a yawn. "But now, let's all head to bed before Eden falls asleep with her face in her dessert."

Before they stood to go, Suzette spoke up, "Wait, please. It is so wonderful to have you three here and together. So… Isaac, Walter, and I have something to share with you as well, if you can spare another minute or two. I am sorry Eden, I see how fatigued you are, but this will not take long, I promise."

Eden smiled and said, "Please go on. I can certainly stay awake long enough to listen."

Suzette's smile widened, and her eyes sparkled. "We have discussed that the three of you have a lot of changes happening in your lives right now, and perhaps adding even more change to that would not only be unnecessary, it might be detrimental."

"Does this have to do with us getting married?" Nico asked.

"Mm, in a way it does, yes," she answered. "We think that the three of you need to concentrate on your new jobs. Nicolo is to work full-time in the clinic for the first time ever, Eden is hopefully going to be a wife to two men," she gave Matty a pointed look, and he smiled back at her, "and a mother, and Matty, now we are delighted to hear that you will take on a new position teaching bright young men and impacting their lives in a good way. You all need to learn how to navigate an unusual marriage, and one thing you don't need to worry about is where you are going to be living. Eden, you can benefit from the assistance of all of us with your new baby, and you won't need to run a household at the same time. And to be perfectly frank, not one of you is financially ready for a new house, even with the best deal New West Builders can give you. This house of ours is so large, we have more than enough room, and to me it will be like living back in France at my father's chateau with my family and my older brother's family under one roof. My grandmother also lived with us for several years."

"Also," Isaac added, "another thing about remaining here is that there may come a time when one or more of you feels the need to maintain a certain level of privacy about your relationship. We think you'll be able to achieve that better here than you might living in your own home with just the three of you. Here, you look like part of a big household. On your own, you may attract more attention. I wish that were not so, but it seems people are naturally nosy about other folks and their private business."

Suzette asked, "So, what do you all think? Will you forget the notion of moving away and stay here?"

Eden was the first to respond, saying, "That is wonderfully generous of you. Personally, I love the idea."

"Maman, Pa, Papa, thank you," Nico said with love in his eyes. "It's a wonderful idea. I was worried about Eden especially since I might have long or late hours unexpectedly, and now I know she will have plenty of help and company, even while Matty is off at work. And I know also that Matty needs reassurance by being surrounded by family."

Matty had a soft, loving expression on his face when he answered, "I wish I had more to contribute. You all have given me so much. Thank you for the wonderful offer. I also love the idea. I just have to solidify a few things in my life before I can commit to anything. I'm sure you all understand."

Isaac spoke up and answered, "Matty, just love them. That's all we would like to see from you. And be the man you were meant to be. You owe us nothing. We can't tell you often enough that you are like a son to us, and we hope you will stay where you are loved, and where you belong."

Walter smiled contentedly. "Now all of you go to bed before Eden collapses. We understand you have many adjustments to make. Be open and not afraid to love."

That reminded Nico. "Papa, I meant to ask, did you or Pa find a cooperative judge in Los Angeles yet? One who would agree to marry the three of us?"

"Not yet, son. We'll keep trying."

Isaac added, "If you all determine that you would like a larger bed, please let me know, and I'll get busy having one built for you right away. We can also remodel Nico's old room for you to better accommodate three people. But we'll talk about that later. Now… good night, loved ones."

Nico thanked his pa and offered his hand to Eden. The three of them headed down the hall to their bedroom. As they walked, Matty said thoughtfully, "It's interesting that they all presume to know we'll be together permanently, even though we haven't made it official in any way."

"Oh, Matty," Nico laughed. "They know us. There isn't any other way we can live."

"Lucky me," Eden sighed. "I had no idea what was in store when this handsome man plowed into me because he was trying to read a pamphlet and walk through a door at the same time."

"That sounds like something Walter would do," Matty observed.

Nico nodded sagely. Indeed it did.

Entering his room, Nico asked, "If they can't find us a judge, what do the two of you want to do to get married?"

Eden smiled dreamily at him and answered, "Nico, dearest man, I am way too happy to worry about that right now, and I am dying to make love to you both. May we table that conversation for tomorrow?"

Both men looked at her hungrily. Matty nodded in agreement and Nico said, "Of course. Let's get rid of all these clothes then, shall we?" They started with Eden. Four hands began to undress her carefully. When she could access them, she would undo a few buttons of a man's shirt or trousers. In this way, they were all disrobed fairly quickly. Matty took a more active role in this process this time, Nico noticed. Perhaps he was getting closer to a commitment because he had fewer worries weighing him down. Or perhaps he was simply glad to see them after being separated for several days. Either way, Nico took it as a good sign.

Eden was the first to speak up when they all stood in the middle of the room with nothing on. She was between the two men, and they were both slowly kissing and fondling her.

Clearing her throat, she asked, "Matty, have you ever done to Nico what he's done to you?"

The men's heads snapped up, and Nico looked a little surprised. Matty looked amused. "I have not, but if he's willing, I would love to try it."

"Well, that was one suggestion I had, but I also have another."

"Our lady is full of ideas, it seems," Nico whispered in her ear.

"Yes, but they are ideas *you* put there."

"Even better," he said with a laugh. "What is it?"

"Remember when you simulated what it might be like if Matty were inside of me at the same time as you? And you used your fingers to simulate him? I want that."

Matty sucked in a deep breath. "Great plan, Nico," he said and bent over to kiss Nico enthusiastically. When that was over, he asked, "May I do her backside?"

"Sure, but Eden, Matty is a lot bigger than my fingers, so we'll go slowly and do this carefully."

She gave an involuntary shiver. "I can't wait," she whispered.

"First, we'll have to get you nice and relaxed, so lie back on the bed, and we'll take turns feasting on that pretty clitoris of yours until you see stars."

"Yes, please."

"Then you can sit on my face, and I'll keep driving you

wild while Matty prepares that rosebud of yours for his big cock. This is going to be fun."

After two lovely climaxes done exactly the way Nico suggested, Eden felt positively boneless. Moving into a new position, she continued to get oral pleasure from Nico while Matty was quite careful and thorough with her bottom. She loved every minute of it—as evidenced by her moans and groans.

After she shuddered her way through yet another ecstatic spasm, Nico directed her, "Slide down onto me… Ahh!" he moaned as his voice cracked. "You'll have to wait a moment, Eden. Matty has my cock in his mouth and ohh… that feels *so* good."

Matty chuckled with a mouth full of Nico as he swirled his tongue around and sucked. He popped off and drew Eden's hips down Nico's body. Holding firmly onto Nico's cock, Matty guided her into position and helped her slide down onto him. "That is the most beautiful sight. I wish you could both see what I'm seeing right now," he told them reverently. "Nico, you're so hard and eager, and Eden, your hole is relaxed and ready for me. This is incredible."

He watched them gyrate a moment as he happily greased up his own erection with olive oil. "Here I come, Eden. I hope you love this. If it's too much, just say so."

"Do it," she commanded in a strangled voice. "Now! I need you, Matty!" Then she whispered, "I love you, Nico. You've given me something so few women will ever get to have." Then she let out an enormous gasp as Matty's big cock breached her for the first time. "Oh! Now you've both taken my virginity in different ways," she giggled softly, but the giggles melted into panting and moaning as Matty started to prod and retreat rhythmically. "Oh this… this is… I don't even know what to call it, but we need to do this over and over!"

"I can feel you, Matty," groaned Nico. "Eden is right. This is incredible. I'm inside of the woman I love, and I'm rubbing against the man I love at the same time. This is perfection." He squeezed his hand in between their bodies so he could manipulate her clit, delighting at the sight of Eden squirming and shuddering with bliss. She also began to squeeze and release him with her inner muscles until he couldn't take the pleasure anymore. He let out a long moan as he poured what felt like his soul into her in hot, sticky spurts.

Matty couldn't last long after he saw how excited Nico was. He began to pump harder into Eden, and as soon as her muscles clenched and her breathing altered, he let loose with the most incredible stream of cum he'd ever imagined. It was a transcendental experience. This was it. This was how he was meant to live. With these two people who loved each other so fiercely and still needed him to make themselves feel complete. "Oh my God, I love you two," he moaned as he emptied himself into Eden's body. He kissed her neck and shoulders and then craned around and kissed Nico deeply.

"Good to know, Matty," Nico whispered with a satisfied grin.

♡♡♡

OVER THE NEXT FEW DAYS, THE HOW-TO-DO-IT CONVERSATION went on and on. Nico, however, had to start work in Doc Louis' clinic, so he wasn't available for much of the discussion. That left the questions and planning to Eden and Matty.

The two of them made some interesting discoveries.

Twenty~Four

Doc Louis was ecstatic with Nico's medical proficiency and the modern knowledge he brought to the clinic. He told Nico, "Over the next six months or so, I plan to help out in a secondary role to you, and gradually I will do less and less so I can spend more time with my lovely Marguerite while I still have my faculties intact. I am not getting any younger, you know. We will have to determine whether the workload is too much for you, and you might want to start thinking about hiring my replacement."

Nico brightened up at that and answered, "I have just the man—Otto Schubert. He was one of my fellow students whom I admired tremendously, and he didn't seem too happy to be returning to Idaho. He's extremely bright and wonderfully personable with patients. They all seemed to trust him implicitly. I'll write to him straight away and see if he'd like to join us here. Also, Eden has made some inquiries with her friends from nursing school, and she ought to hear back from them soon. We might have more help than we need if everyone is interested."

"Oh, Nico, you can never have too much help around here. While you were gone, the practice became so busy I could barely wait for your return. People are always going to get hurt and be sick, and this city is growing every day. Let us get some help and do it soon. We might also think about expanding the property or moving to a larger location."

So, as the letters from nurses arrived, and two of them expressed an interest and availability, offers for interviews were sent back immediately.

Otto Schubert answered back from Idaho that he could be there in a month. Nico was thrilled to hear that. He was already feeling the stress of overwork, and he'd just begun. Professionally, however, he was as happy as a clam at high water. He loved the challenge of his new medical practice.

♡♡♡

MATTY CONTINUED TO BE CONCERNED ABOUT THE DIOCESE and the debt he owed them if he were to quit being a deacon and not go through with becoming a priest.

"Why don't we pay whoever is in charge a visit and straighten things out?" Eden asked.

"Bishop Morrow is in charge of the Los Angeles diocese.

I've certainly heard Father Andrew invoke his name often enough. It might not be a bad idea to go speak with him, but why would you want to come?"

"Matty, first of all, I like spending time with you, and second, whatever you find out will have an impact on not only you, but also on Nico and me. Is there a reason you wouldn't want me there with you? If you don't, I'll keep out of it. Or I'll come along for moral support, if you like. It's completely up to you."

Matty reached up and stroked Eden's cheek. Looking into her eyes, he answered, "Normally, I would answer that I need to do this on my own, but I find I have this growing need to be with you as much as possible. So, if you really want to accompany me, I will gladly accept the offer." He kissed her sweetly and then pulled back saying, "I don't even feel guilty kissing my best friend's fiancée. What has become of me?"

"I don't feel guilty either. I feel just right." They both laughed and she said, "Let's go see the man."

"Maybe I should first call for an appointment," Matty answered.

An hour later, the two of them were headed downtown to the bishop's office, but not before Matty changed back into his clerical attire. "I think for this meeting, I need to do this," he explained.

♡♡♡

"FATHER DEACON MATTHEW REMINGTON, HOW GOOD TO MEET you at last. I understand that condolences are in order. I was sorry to hear from Father Andrew that your father passed recently."

"Thank you, your Excellency."

"And who is this lovely young woman accompanying you?"

"I'd like to introduce Eden Godwin… the fiancée of my best friend, and a most dear friend of mine as well."

The bishop held out his hand, and Eden was suddenly struck with the worry of what to do. Was she supposed to kiss his ring? Shaking her head inwardly, she took his hand and gave him a firm handshake, saying, "I'm pleased to meet you, Bishop Morrow." If he expected someone to kiss his ring, he needed to speak to someone who wasn't raised Lutheran, she told herself. Besides, Matty hadn't kissed anything.

His facial expression didn't reveal whether or not she'd made a faux pas as he exclaimed, "Eden Godwin. What a lovely name your parents blessed you with."

"Thank you, your… uh… sir."

"Please, have a seat, and would either of you like some coffee? I can have some brought in right away."

"No thank you, sir," Matty answered. "We don't want to take up a lot of your valuable time and sincerely appreciate you taking a moment to speak with us today. I have a few questions that have been preying on my mind, sir."

"That's most understandable, young man, especially as we

are so near to the date when you are scheduled to take your final vows. I am slightly confused, however, why you came directly to me and not to your personal confessor, Father Andrew. He knows you so well, and he's had a vested interest in your continued success on the road to becoming a priest. He has kept me updated on your stellar progress throughout your education, and I congratulate you for that. Father Andrew has also repeatedly assured me that were he to advance in the Hierarchy of Order to become, say, a bishop upon my retirement or advancement, that his parish would be in excellent hands with you."

"That's just it, sir. Father Andrew may be too personally invested. I have repeatedly expressed severe doubts about taking final vows. I'm afraid he's not listening to me. I apologize for taking up your time with this matter, but I'm not getting anywhere with him."

The bishop's face showed a momentary shock, and then he schooled his featured back into an inscrutable mask. "Interesting. Please go on."

"I hope my coming here isn't unprofessional, but what I wanted to speak to you about is that he has told me over and over that I have a huge debt I owe the diocese for having paid all of my tuition and living expenses for the past several years. I was led to believe that my debt even preceded seminary, though now I understand that the earlier grades were actually tuition free. In any case, I need to know how much I owe back to the diocese if—" Matty hesitated and glanced at Eden before squaring his shoulders and correcting himself, "actually, *when* I take a position as a teacher rather than as a priest. I want to teach in a lay capacity, not as a deacon. The Vincentian fathers have offered me a job at their boys' school here in Los Angeles."

"And what is to preclude you from becoming a priest if you plan to teach at a parochial school anyway? I don't think I see the problem."

Matty hung his head for a second to gather his thoughts. He took a deep breath and looked the bishop in the eye. "I cannot live a celibate life. I am deeply and irrevocably in love, you see, Excellency. I have deep faith, and I love the church, but I cannot serve my community as a priest or even as a deacon. In fact, I have never expressed an interest in becoming a priest, but I have felt compelled to do so by duty because of the debt I have to pay."

"Well. That's something, isn't it?" Bishop Morrow nodded thoughtfully. "It's not unheard of for a young man to have second thoughts about taking the final step to become a priest. Perhaps you need more time to pray and reflect on your decision before making it final."

"No, Excellency. This debt was placed on me as a child, and I never felt I had a choice—I just felt trapped. Now that I am an adult, I cannot go through with it, and I am tremendously sorry to the diocese for letting anyone down."

"I see. Well, I'm sorry if this experience has given you grief. Taking final vows is supposed to be a joyous occasion in one's life, not a life sentence of frustration and doubt. But I must explain something to you that I'm surprised you didn't know. All seminarians have their tuition paid by their local diocese. Some areas are obviously wealthier than others, so some dioceses can be more generous than the poorer areas, and you come from the wealthiest in all of California. Your tuition and simple living expenses were not a burden to anyone, and I deeply regret that you may have been led to believe otherwise. If a seminarian leaves the program and does not become a priest, sometimes they are asked to repay half of the tuition, but we don't have that stipulation here in Los Angeles. We are satisfied that we have sponsored a bright young man who will go on to serve his community in some positive way, priest or no. You will still be a tremendous asset to the Catholic Church as a lay teacher, and we are proud to have been able to provide you with the means to do so."

Matty blinked for a moment, clearly surprised. Finally, he croaked, "Excellency, are you serious?"

Bishop Morrow chuckled. "I am not exactly known for telling fabrications, young man."

"No, sir. I didn't mean to imply…"

"Of course you didn't. I just have to assume that the subject never came up in seminary among your peers because everyone was in the same boat, so to speak. If money isn't an issue, it's not often discussed, especially when you all had so many fascinating topics to discuss with your studies. You did enjoy the education at least, I hope?"

Matty beamed at the Bishop. "Yes, sir, I truly did enjoy it. I love learning about religion and history. I've had a recent follow-up conversation with the boys' college, and if I accept their offer, they want me to teach Latin and religious history in the fall. I'm looking forward to it. Seminary gave me the perfect background to teach what I enjoy."

"Well, that's splendid. And I wish you well. I just have to wonder why Father Andrew was less than forthcoming with you about your supposed debt to society, especially when you'll be contributing in a positive way."

"Oh, well, Father Andrew doesn't know about the offer from St. Vincent's. He hasn't been accessible for me to discuss anything with him lately. I'm afraid he's been avoiding me, actually, sir."

"Well, that's a bit odd. I think a conversation with him is in order. But don't worry. He'll come around when he hears you'll be serving Los Angeles Catholics in a positive way. He'll just have to find a new protégé if he wants to mentor his own replacement. It's not easy finding someone who wants to become a priest and who is qualified to do so. He probably felt he'd found a gold mine in you and didn't want to consider the alternative. Now, I have another appointment, so I'll have to say goodbye. It was a pleasure meeting you and Miss Godwin. I wish you both the best of luck in your futures, and may God bless you."

"Excellency, I just have one more quick question, if you don't mind." Bishop Morrow nodded, so he continued, "My friends Nico and Eden would like me to preside over their wedding. Is it acceptable for me to be the officiant knowing that I plan to resign from my position as deacon? I don't want to act in any insincere fashion or cause their marriage to be null for any reason."

"I see no problem with your participation. You are still a deacon with all of the privileges that provides until I receive a written letter of resignation from you." He looked at Eden and said, "May you have a long and happy marriage. Now, I must go."

They all stood, and Eden suppressed a sudden desire to curtsy to the man. Instead, they both thanked him and shook his hand once more. When they left his office, Eden wanted to squeal with joy and throw herself into Matty's arms, but she straightened her posture and walked as sedately as she possibly could. She knew it wouldn't do to throw herself at a man in a clerical collar outside of a church, so she whispered in his ear instead, "Take me home and make love to me. Now!"

"Oh, Eden, I've never felt so relieved in my life! Let's go!" They hopped into the carriage and off they went—home to the Stark-James estate. "I can't wait to get out of these clothes for once and for all."

Eden smiled and whispered, "I can't wait to get you out of them either. Too bad Nico is at the clinic today. We'll just have to pretend he's with us."

UNAWARE THAT ANY OF THIS WAS HAPPENING WITH MATTY, Nico was hard at work at the clinic. He had interviews arranged with two potential nurses and was happy to share with Doc Louis that his friend Otto would be joining their staff in the near future. He'd worked hard during medical school, but that was nothing compared to the responsibilities he had at the clinic. He had been going home exhausted but feeling great at the same time.

On this particular day, Nico was heading down the hall when he heard a familiar voice praying over a seriously ill female patient. Father Andrew had apparently been summoned by the patient's husband or children. He waited politely for the prayer to end, and when he heard the word "amen," he stuck his head in the door and said, "Afternoon, Father Andrew. It's good of you to come."

Strangely, Father Andrew merely raised his head and glared at Nico. He snubbed his greeting and went back to his praying.

Nico found this response odd since the priest had always been cordial to everyone in his family in the past. He thought perhaps he'd interrupted something and suddenly felt like a fool. He stepped away from the door and resolved to apologize as soon as possible. He went immediately into the exam room of the next patient to check on the man's wound. About the same time he finished dressing the wound, he heard footsteps in the hallway and excused himself after instructing the patient to keep the wound clean.

"Father Andrew, a word please?" Nico blocked the hallway and gestured into his private office as he stood in front of the priest, giving him little choice but to follow his direction.

Getting right to it as soon as he closed the door, Nico said, "Father, I apologize if I interrupted your pastoral visit with Mrs. Carpenter. Your presence is always a comfort, I'm sure, to the patients and their families." So far Father Andrew had yet to smile or even nod, so Nico continued, "I'm glad you're here because I've been wanting to ask you if you would agree to officiating my marriage to my fiancée, Eden." Nico was fairly certain at this point that he wasn't going to find anyone to marry all three of them, and he worried Matty might find it emotionally difficult to conduct the ceremony, so he'd best get on with things and marry Eden. They would figure out what to do with Matty on their own, but he knew how anxious Eden was to get married.

"Is she Catholic?" was his terse reply.

"No, sir. Lutheran."

"The only way I will preside is if she agrees to convert."

"I'm sorry. I don't see why that's necessary. She's a baptized Christian. How long would it take to convert, if she were to agree?"

"A year or two." This wasn't exactly true because the conversion for a practicing Christian could be accomplished in as few as a couple of weeks, but Father Andrew did not feel like being accommodating on this day.

"Eden doesn't want to wait that long to get married. Thank you anyway, but I guess we'll have to find an alternate solution." He studied Father Andrew's petulant expression and asked, "Is there something else wrong, Father? What am I missing?"

"You are ruining everything!" he snapped.

"Sir? What exactly am I ruining? Do you disapprove of my taking over the clinic? I assure you I am completely qualified and have Doc Louis' full confidence. We also have some wonderful plans to add staff and expand the practice..."

"That's not what I'm talking about, you conceited brat!" he interrupted as Nico gaped at him. "You've turned Father Matthew away from me! He was *mine* to mold and mine to..."

"Matty is his own person, Father. He doesn't belong to anyone," Nico interrupted right back. "I haven't done anything except love him and encourage him to decide his own path. My entire family loves him. You know that."

Father Andrew snorted. "Love him. Hah. You don't know the meaning of the word."

"Pardon me?"

"You think because your family coddles him and tries to interfere in his true calling, you love him. *I'm* the one who truly loves him! I've watched him suffer and struggle for years, all the time keeping the purest faith in the Almighty. He has the most beautiful soul in the world. But you think because you show up to mass once or twice a year, you know what it's like to be a good Catholic. You and your heathen parents who lead the most immoral lifestyle imaginable—you think you know how to love? Hah! You are all a bunch of corrupt sinners, and I pity this fiancée of yours who's getting dragged into your family's depravity!"

Nico was beyond stunned by this outburst. Instead of raising his voice, however, he asked quietly, "Father Andrew, what has happened to you? You've always been a friend to my family, and it was their impression that you accepted them with grace and understanding. Now you call them names and accuse us of trying to manipulate a person I've grown up with and love as dearly as I love my parents and my fiancée. How were you able to dine at their table over and over and then go home and look at yourself in the mirror? If you reviled them all so much, how can you be such a hypocrite? And why have you been avoiding Matty when all he's wanted to do was talk to you? You confuse me, sir."

Father Andrew, who'd been standing with his chest puffed out, suddenly collapsed into a chair and moaned, "It's all falling apart. All of my careful plans. Everything was going along just fine until you came back. You showed up with that woman." He glared at Nico. "You tempted him with your sinning ways and turned him against *me* and the beautiful, loving partnership *we* could have had. I waited patiently, you know. He was too young, so I waited until he was a grown man, and I knew he'd be ready for me." There was a strange, almost mad twinkle in Father Andrew's eyes as he continued, "I had it all figured out. It's a lonely life, the priesthood. But it doesn't have to be. Not if you have someone you can rely on. Someone you can come home to. Someone you can... work through your temptations with. Sin can be absolved, as long as you are sorry. As long as you know it's a sin. That's what's wrong with your family, Nico. You don't have any shame! And now you're pulling Matty away from me, away from what we could be..."

Trying to keep the shock out of his voice over this revelation, Nico said, "You're jealous! Father Andrew, you can't seriously think you could somehow force Matty to love you just because you want him to." Receiving nothing but an angry stare from Father Andrew, he continued, "Well, I can't presume to speak for Matty because this is his business, but I sincerely recommend that you come to the house and talk to him yourself. You can't keep hiding from him. I believe you owe an apology to my parents for taking advantage of their hospitality while judging them, and you owe Matty an apology for trying to run his life for him. And something else, which has been bothering me for some time… why would you tell Matty you hadn't given his father last rites? You know that hurt him far more deeply than he let on."

"He needed to feel a little of *my* pain." Father Andrew stood and bolted from the office and out of the clinic.

"Whew," Nico said, shaking his head. "Wait until Matty hears this."

♡♡♡

THE DOCKET OF PATIENTS WAS BLESSEDLY LIGHT FOR THE REST of the day, and Nico was able to head home early. He desperately wanted to bathe and get into comfortable clothes, so after a quick greeting to his mother, he headed straight for his room. Opening the bedroom door, he smiled to see Eden and Matty wrapped around each other and sound asleep. On closer inspection, he realized they were both naked under the blanket. He nodded happily and quietly headed to take a bath, thinking, *Good for them. They needed this.* He didn't feel an ounce of jealousy, he realized, and smiled again.

A little while later, Matty awoke to the sound of Eden making appreciative noises in his embrace, and he saw that Nico had joined them. He was immediately torn between making love and telling Nico about the interesting conversation they'd had with the bishop. *Well, first things first.* He kissed both of his lovers, and they proceeded to explore one another in the most interesting ways possible. Mouths and hands were everywhere, and the sounds of passion filled the room. Finally, he asked softly, "Nico, may I take you this time?"

Eden's eyes sparkled, and she smiled as Nico thought it over.

Nico answered with a lopsided grin, "I never thought I'd feel like the virgin amongst us. Yes, Matty. Please do."

"You'll enjoy it," Matty promised. "And I'll be careful."

"I know you will. I trust you. Eden had no complaints, did you, love?" He kissed her cheek.

"None at all. It feels very naughty, though. Now, make love to me, Nico, while Matty gets you ready."

Several minutes later, Eden was enjoying Nico's steady thrusts into her body when she heard him gasp loudly and throw back his head as if in complete abandon. Matty was behind Nico and had obviously claimed Nico's backside. Matty's face was a study in concentration as he began thrusting in and out of Nico, and Nico could not suppress a case of the shudders as this assault on his senses continued. He gripped the bed on either side of Eden and let Matty control the speed and rhythm of their lovemaking. Harder and harder, Matty pounded into Nico and Nico into Eden until Eden nearly screamed with the incredible sensation that poured through her. One after the other of them succumbed to their passion until they all lay in a satisfied heap.

"Did you like it, Nico?" Eden asked when her breathing returned to normal.

"Oh, God yes. Making love to both of you at the same time is amazing."

Matty chuckled. "It is. Now… will you both marry me?"

Nico rolled so he could look at both of them at once and said, "You know we will."

"Absolutely," Eden added. "How?"

"I have an idea." Matty told them. "How about this? If I preside over your wedding vows to each other, you two can be legally married as you originally planned. Then, as part of the ceremony, we can all three participate in a handfasting ceremony."

"What's that?" Eden asked.

"It's an old Celtic ritual that goes back at least two thousand years. The Vikings also had a version of it in their culture. The marriage couple has someone wrap their hands together with a ribbon or whatever you choose, and they make promises to one another. Although the tradition has been practiced by many cultures since its beginning, it's probably not legally binding in California. It's definitely good enough for me though, as it is emotionally as binding as a legal marriage. The more modern belief is that if the union lasts for more than a year and a day after the handfasting, it will last forever. We could have one—or even all three—of your parents wrap our hands, Nico. What do you both think?"

"Oh, Matty, that would be beautiful," Eden said with tears in her eyes.

"How soon can we do it?" Nico asked.

"As soon as the two of you get a marriage license, and we figure out the vows we each want to make. I propose we do it right here in the courtyard of the estate since this house is so special to all of us. I can't think of a better place; it's peaceful and beautiful out there with all of the bougainvillea and the fountain." He looked down and then back up. "I don't think the church is exactly where the three of us should do this."

"About that…" Nico started. "I talked to Father Andrew today, and he made some rather eye-opening revelations."

Matty nodded and said, "I'm not surprised. Eden and I met with Bishop Morrow this afternoon, and we also received some interesting and somewhat startling information."

Eden interjected, "It's almost time for dinner, so why don't we get dressed and share all of this with everyone at the same time?"

"Great idea," Nico agreed.

"Yes," Matty said firmly.

"I told Father Andrew to come to the house tonight to talk to you and my parents about his behavior, but I doubt he'll show up." Nico shrugged. "He hasn't yet, but we'll see. Maybe he'll man up. Probably not."

CHAPTER

Twenty~Six

D INNER CONVERSATION THAT NIGHT WAS BOTH EYE-OPENING and revealing. They discussed everything that transpired with the bishop and Father Andrew.

"It's such a relief to know I don't have any actual monetary debts after all," Matty said. "And Bishop Morrow stressed that I'll be using my seminary education to benefit the community anyway, so he's satisfied. But Father Andrew sounds a bit like he's going off his rocker from what you say, Nico."

"I don't know," replied Nico with a grin. "You're an easy person to love. I feel a little sorry for the man and his unrequited adoration."

"Thank you, but…" Matty looked perplexed. "He really said he was waiting for me to grow up?"

"He did. And I got the definite impression that the man is

not all that concerned with celibacy. His interest in you is not what I'd call 'pure.'"

"Well, I'm sorry for the man," Matty said sincerely. "I never saw that coming, and it must give him pain to want what he can't have—for several reasons."

Eden muttered something under her breath.

Suzette got her dander up when she realized Father Andrew disapproved of her marriage to Isaac and Walter while pretending to be their friend. "He is supposed to accept people for who they are. Jesus taught us that, did he not? What a terrible hypocrite. He was just here for the cuisine and to get close to Matty!" Then she swore softly in French, making Nico squelch a laugh. She huffed and turned to her husbands, kissing one and then the other. "It doesn't matter what that ridiculous man thinks. We are happy and have a beautiful, loving family. *That* is what is important."

Isaac interjected thoughtfully, "I find it interesting we all focused on the possibility that Father Andrew was ambitious about his career when all along his motive was to be with Matty more. The man clearly misses the clues that our young man here has no interest in him, and he's gone about this in a strange way. He's also a terribly big phony for a man who ought to be a paragon of virtue. All of this lying doesn't say much for the kind of priest he is, either."

"Jealousy and frustration can drive a person to do strange things, as we've seen," Walter opined.

Eden asked, "Why would he keep avoiding Matty though if he actually wanted to be with him?

Isaac smiled kindly. "I'm sure he didn't want to face Matty's lack of interest. He'd had years of imagining a wonderful union when Matty grew up, only to realize it wasn't going to happen. He didn't want the positive proof of that. I wonder how aware of this the bishop is; that man sounds pretty shrewd."

"I got the sense," Matty answered, "that Bishop Morrow keeps his cards close to his vest. I wouldn't be surprised if he had a long chat with Father Andrew to set him straight on several things."

Walter told them, "On a more practical note, I have to go to the courthouse first thing in the morning to file a license for a new building project. If you like, I can give you a ride over. You can get a marriage license at the same time."

Eden beamed at him. "Thank you. That would be wonderful." Nico squeezed her hand, and Matty kissed her cheek. "I feel like we're finally making some progress."

"What day would you like to have the wedding?" Suzette asked. "I need to make plans!"

"Please, nothing extravagant," Eden asked. "I would prefer immediate family and just a few close friends if you can keep it to that."

"Watch out, dearest. That can still be a large number of people. Our family alone sometimes feels like a cast of thousands," Nico said with a grin.

"I guess I can live with that," she agreed.

THE NEXT DAY, NICO AND EDEN ACCOMPANIED WALTER downtown and took care of the necessary paperwork for their upcoming nuptials. Nico couldn't resist giving Eden a big kiss on the courthouse steps, eliciting a few whistles from passing pedestrians. "The neighbors probably see this kind of thing all the time when couples get their licenses here," he told Eden as she broke out into a fit of giggles. They headed off in high spirits.

Reminiscing happily about his own nuptials to Suzette and Isaac as he drove, Walter dropped Nico off at the clinic and took Eden back to the house to work on plans with Suzette and her best friends Adeline and Marguerite. When Suzette's friends discovered that Eden and Nico would be including Matty in the wedding ceremony with a handfasting—and not just as the officiant—they were beside themselves with glee.

"You will never regret this decision," Adeline declared. She was married to Jasper and Royal and thought a three-person union was the best thing ever. "We are very, very lucky women, Eden. Welcome to the club." She gave her a wink.

Marguerite presented Eden with a gown, saying, "I could not resist, cherie. There is no charge. It was a pet project for me. If you do not care for it, do not worry. My heart will stay intact."

Eden was speechless for a moment as she took in the magnificent dress. Then tears formed in her eyes, and she exclaimed, "I have never had anything so beautiful in my life. Thank you, Marguerite, from the bottom of my heart. I'll cherish this forever." She threw her arms around the older woman.

"Do not thank me until you see how it looks on you. I thought it would bring out the color of your pretty eyes."

"I love it so much. I just hope to do it justice."

MATTY DECIDED THAT HE WOULD TAKE SOME TIME TO VISIT ST. Vincent's College for Boys and give them his final acceptance of the position they were offering. When he completed his paperwork, he asked if he could take a quick look at the classroom he'd be assigned to. Upon doing so, he discovered that it was currently unoccupied, so he couldn't resist entering and sitting at the teacher's desk in the front of the room for a moment. A tremendous feeling of calm and rightness settled over him like a warm blanket as he imagined future lively conversations and possible humorous pranks from young men with eager minds. He said a little prayer for the ability to keep his students engaged every day.

Matty left the school in a terrific mood, even though he was weighed down with a heavy pile of textbooks. He barely felt them, he was so buoyed with joy. He walked back to the estate in a state of pure contentment. Everything around him looked colorful and smelled sweet.

He felt certain he'd recently made the best decisions of his life.

When he arrived at the estate, Eden was already there. After talking with the older ladies about wedding plans and subsequently trying on her new gown, she was glowing with happiness.

"Matty, you're lucky you got to be around Nico and his family while you were a child. Ever since I've been here, wonderful things keep happening. It's as if all the love in this house creates little miracles. Nico brought me to you, and now I find I love you the same way I love him. Who would ever expect that? And I feel like part of this incredible family in this beautiful city. We're having a baby, and he or she will grow up with loving parents and grandparents all around. I didn't realize I even had this much capacity for love. It's... I don't even know how to express the depths of my joy."

Matty wrapped her in his arms and held her tightly to his heart. "I know just what you mean. This home has always felt like my sanctuary. I have loved Nico for as long as I can remember, and I never expected to love another person until I laid eyes on you. And a baby! My heart is full to bursting with love for you, for Nico, and for the little person we will all be able to raise together. I feel like I've come out of a long, cold, and very dark tunnel into the brilliant sunshine. Life is good,

Eden. God had a better plan for me after all." He kissed her sweetly.

FOUR DAYS LATER, THE WEDDING FINALLY HAPPENED, AND THE three young lovers could not have been happier.

The house bustled with activity, and during the morning, extra flowers were brought in to embellish the already gorgeous setting. As the appointed time drew near, the courtyard filled up with colorfully dressed friends and family members, making the entire area resemble a tableau for a magnificent painting. Nico's talented brothers and sisters sat to one side with their instruments and provided a wonderful string quartet to complete the perfect atmosphere.

Suzette had to hire extra help to handle the meal service that would happen after the ceremony. The kitchen looked like controlled chaos where their talented cook had been preparing for this event for all four days—ever since she'd been given the word. Now she was barking orders left and right at her newly enlisted helpers.

Even with just close friends and family, the wedding would be serving about seventy-five people. So much for a small gathering. It couldn't be helped, Eden was assured. Too many people loved the Stark-James family and wanted to share their joy.

Matty couldn't contain his huge smile as he stood in front

of the fountain waiting for Nico and Eden to join him. He wore a tailored black suit, but instead of a clerical collar, he had on a brilliant white shirt. Eden and Nico thought he looked dashingly handsome that way.

Suzette and her friends had helped Eden dress and style her hair, and she was the most stunning bride Nico and Matty could ever imagine. Her gown was perfection, but mostly it was her happiness—the smile that sparkled in her eyes—that made her so incredibly lovely.

Nico also had a fine new suit, and his blond curls were trimmed and tamed for the occasion. All the unmarried—and a few married—ladies in attendance secretly eyed Eden with envy. He was a dashing groom, and the eager way he looked at Eden made the female guests positively swoon.

When Matty finished the traditional wedding ceremony, having Nico and Eden recite their vows and declaring by the power vested in him that they were now man and wife, some of the guests wondered why Matty didn't invite the groom to kiss his bride immediately.

Instead, Suzette, Isaac, and Walter approached the three young people with long, colorful ribbons in their hands.

Nico, Eden, and Matty then made a triangle, Nico clasping Eden's right wrist, Eden closing that hand around Matty's right wrist, and Matty taking Nico's right wrist, sealing the three-sided shape with all of them connected equally and united as one. Nico's parents, one at a time, wrapped a ribbon around them, binding the three of them together as one unit.

All six of the participants were smiling and looking as happy as can be.

Just as Walter was tying his ribbon, a priest marched purposefully through the front door of the estate. A harried servant who was new and unfamiliar with the family spotted him. She didn't know what was happening in the courtyard and became worried that the officiant must be running late and holding up the ceremony.

Taking initiative, the servant rushed the priest to the door to the courtyard, shoved him through, and scurried back to the kitchen. She shook her head and tutted to herself at how ridiculous it was for a priest to be so tardy to a wedding. After all, the guests had been seated for some time now and must have been tired of waiting for the man.

Matty was opening his mouth to say something pithy and wonderful about the symbolism of handfasting and the solid strength of a balanced tripod when a loud, angry voice shouted over him, "What is the meaning of this, Father Matthew? I'll have you excommunicated!"

CHAPTER
Twenty~Seven

Eden looked horrified as she regarded this austere man who was ruining the happiest moment of her life.

Nico wanted to pull away and thrash Father Andrew for his outburst and for barging in and spoiling their special vows, but he was tied fast to his two lovers. There was no way he could break away, so he glared at the priest. Later, he would reflect that it was probably a good thing.

Matty, however, burst into peals of laughter, causing everyone to stare at him openmouthed.

"What's so funny?" Eden whispered. "He's ruining everything!"

Matty brought himself under control and said in a loud voice, "Welcome to our wedding, Father Andrew. I'm sorry you saw fit to cause a commotion, but if you'd paid attention in seminary the way you ought to have, you'd know that *you* have no more ability to excommunicate me than that honeybee over there buzzing around the daisies. So please, either sit down and enjoy the rest of our wedding like a polite guest or get out of here. Your disruption is not welcome.

"Bishop Morrow is perfectly aware, by the way, that I'm performing this ceremony today, and I even checked with him about incorporating a handfasting as part of the vows. He had no problem with it—even if its roots predate Christianity—and he said he rather liked the symbolism and the promises."

He didn't add that he'd skipped over the detail that he would actually be part of the handfasting himself—he hadn't wanted to take up too much of the bishop's valuable time. Matty also arranged to have a courier pop over to the bishop's office to deliver his resignation before he, Nico, and Eden sealed the deal on their marriage—in bed. The messenger was heading to the bishop's office with the letter in his pocket at this very moment.

"Well... then you're fired!" Father Andrew shouted as Nico's two brothers Warren and Bay set aside their cello and viola. They took the priest firmly by his arms and began to drag him toward the exit.

"Already taken care of, thanks, Father," Matty told him calmly. "My resignation will be tendered to the diocese in mere minutes."

Desperate, Father Andrew cried, "You're making a huge mistake, Matthew! I could show you so much! Give you so much if you just stay with me like we'd planned."

Matty regarded Father Andrew kindly and said in an understanding voice, "I'm sorry. You're wrong, and you've been lying to yourself as much as to everyone around you for years now. I never made any of those plans; it was all in your head. I suggest a nice long trip to the *confessional*, sir. You'll feel much better after that. Now, please, let us get back to our marriage."

"Come on, Bay," Warren said. "Let's get him out of here." And off they went, hoisting him off the ground so his feet had no purchase. He scrambled to get his footing, but they swiftly marched him out of the courtyard and through the front gate. Bay locked it as Father Andrew stood hollering all sorts of rude insults to them about their depraved family and their disgusting younger brother.

Breaking down in tears, the priest finally shuffled away.

"Poor deluded man," Warren muttered. "Let's hurry back so we can finish our music. But you'll need to unlock that before anyone tries to leave."

Just then, Jeb Hawkins, looking more dapper in a fancy suit than they'd ever seen him, stepped out of the house and offered, "I'll guard the gate for a while, boys. Go back in so you don't miss anything. Some ceremony, eh?"

"It's fine, Jeb. I'm sure Nico would prefer to have you at the wedding," Bay answered, clapping the big man on his shoulder. "I don't think Father Andrew will come at anyone with a gun or try to scale the wall. He's already left anyway, but thanks for the offer." The three of them went back in and locked the front door for good measure.

When the men returned and took their seats, it was to find there was not a dry eye in the congregation. Later, they would hear stories about the beautiful promises Nico, Matty, and Eden made to one another. They had all vowed to love, support, trust, and cherish each other equally and fully for the rest of their lives. They saw themselves, as Matty had started to say when they were interrupted, like the three legs of a tripod—strongest when joined as three.

While realizing that the only legal marriage in the eyes of the state of California was between Nico and Eden, no one had any doubts whatsoever that Matty was any less a part of the marriage on a personal and emotional level. This was a union forever.

The guests raised toast after toast to the three of them. People stumbled over words here and there—so used to referring to the happy "couple"—but they finally settled on calling them the "tripod." The less poetic guests compared them favorably to a three-legged stool. That was accepted with graceful cheer and plenty of laughter.

Royal, however, whispered to Jasper that he was glad no one ever called *them* a three-legged stool with their wife Adeline. "I was glad to get away from milking all of those damned cows. I had enough of those stools!" Then he kissed Jasper's cheek and turned to Adeline, giving her a deep, passionate kiss that made her eyelids flutter. Royal had been raised on a dairy farm and determined early on that it was not his true calling—no matter how the rest of his family felt about it.

The bumbling servant who'd dragged Father Andrew into the ceremony by mistake sought out Suzette and made a groveling apology for her error. Suzette acknowledged that it was an accident and merely told the woman, "Please just be more careful in the future." *Besides*, she thought to herself, *this will give everyone an interesting story to gossip about for years. A wedding no one will soon forget. Ultimately, the only one hurt by it was Father Andrew, and he brought it upon himself by acting like a fool.*

The celebration went on for hours, but finally Eden began to wilt, so her new husbands spirited her away to the wing at the far end of the house. As promised, Isaac had installed a new, much larger bed that accommodated the three of them quite comfortably, and it looked inviting with its soft mattress, fluffy pillows, and silky sheets. But upon entering the room, Eden gathered new strength and alertness.

"I have a surprise for you two," she told the men. They looked at her with interest. "Someone who shall remain nameless whispered into my ear tonight—quite explicitly, I might add. She… oh, I mean *that person* recommended something special for us on our wedding night."

Nico laughed, "Well, that narrows it down to a select few people, Eden. Not too many of our guests would either know of something special we could do or would share anything like that."

"True, but I'm trying to be polite."

Matty wrapped her in his arms from behind and nibbled on her ear, saying, "I like it better when you're being naughty."

"Well, this sounds pretty naughty, and I've been guaranteed that we'll all love it as long as we're careful and use plenty of oil."

"Do tell," Nico prompted as he undid his tie.

As Eden explained what she'd heard, however, both men's jaws dropped.

"And you think that is possible?" Matty asked incredulously.

"She… that person… oh fiddlesticks… it was Marguerite! She swears it is not only possible, it is wonderful. And she promises that everyone we know who's in a three-way union loves it!"

"That's maybe more than I needed to know," Nico laughed. He certainly didn't want to be thinking about his parents on his wedding night. Still… the act sounded pretty incredible. "If you're willing to try it, Eden, I'll go along with you. It would seem to be the hardest for you to manage. I think Matty and I will be fine."

Matty gave a small choking sound and said with a catch in his voice, "More than fine. Are you joking?"

They took extra care getting Eden out of her magnificent gown. "You look so beautiful tonight," Nico told her, "but the less you have on, the more beautiful you are." He winked and helped her hang the gown in her personal wardrobe. An expansion of their room was planned, but it had not yet begun. At least for now, they had enough furniture to accommodate all three of them.

For several minutes, they simply lay on the bed fondling and stroking one another. Kisses landed everywhere, and words of love filled the air. No one was in a rush, although the level of excitement for what they were planning grew and grew. Finally, after the men had brought Eden to a most satisfying climax, they began to stroke her internally with both of their fingers together. Nico kissed and sucked her breasts while Matty played with her sensitive clit. In and out, their joined fingers probed her, feeling how wet and excited she was. With no words, the men pulled out their fingers and entered her again, each with two fingers this time. Eden hissed a little, so they backed off until Matty added some oil to their hands.

"I want one of you in my mouth," she told her men. Nico positioned himself so that he could accommodate her request, and almost lost control as she wrapped her lips around him. He and Matty were still probing her together, and it felt amazing.

Matty then positioned his body so that Nico could take Matty's cock into his mouth.

This made Eden chuckle. She could see how excited the men were. She pulled off Nico with a pop and ordered them breathlessly, "I'm ready for it. Put your big hard cocks into me together now!"

Nico lay on the bed, and Eden positioned herself over him facing away. Carefully, she slid herself down toward his gloriously hard member. She moaned happily as he penetrated her in one long thrust. "Yes, Nico. So good," she moaned. "Now you, Matty."

Matty was so sensitive, he oiled up his cock, but almost couldn't take the pressure of his own hand sliding up and down on himself. He tried to think of something else for a moment other than what he was about to do so he wouldn't embarrass himself before he got inside. He looked down though and saw the most glorious sight of his favorite two people grinding on each other. Nico's cock looked impossibly large going in and out of Eden, and he was supposed to fit himself in there too? He leaned over and sucked Eden's clit, then licked Nico where they were joined, causing them both to shudder with excitement.

"Well, here goes," he said finally.

Matty first slid a finger inside of Eden alongside Nico's cock, and Nico hummed with pleasure at the feel of Matty stroking him. "Yes," he moaned. "More, please!" So Matty added another finger. He continued to stroke Nico inside Eden until he felt that she was sufficiently relaxed to let in his cock as well.

"Do it, Matty. Put your cock in me with Nico's," Eden demanded on a groan.

Matty chuckled. "She gets pretty bossy when she's aroused, doesn't she?"

"Hurry up, Matty," Nico urged. "I want to feel you in here with me. I'm not going to last all night like this. She feels too good."

"Here goes," Matty said, swiping one last smear of oil on himself. Carefully, he fed his erection into Eden in the same place Nico already occupied. At first it didn't seem to fit, but when Nico began to manipulate Eden's clit, she relaxed a bit more, and Matty could see and feel himself sliding inside. "Yes!" he hissed.

"Oh!" Eden cried softly. "It's working! You're both in me together. This feels… amazing and strange all at the same time. I never ever dreamed anything like this could happen."

"Oh, my loves, this is the best thing ever," Nico moaned. "I feel you, Matty, rubbing against me, and I feel Eden's velvet heat surrounding us both together. This is heaven for sure."

"The beautiful garden of Eden?" Matty asked in a choked voice. "Incredible." He began the sensual dance of sliding in and out of Eden, simultaneously stroking his cock against Nico's over and over. Nico kept up his manual manipulation of her clit as he grew more aroused.

Eden shook with a climax as she groaned, "I love you both so much. Everyone needs to experience this much joy! I almost feel selfish having you both to myself." She moaned as another spasm rolled through her senses.

Nico was next. He shot his load, pouring inside of Eden and all over Matty, who could feel Nico's hot seed coating him. This new sensation took him over the top as well, and he nearly cried with the joy and beauty of it. Panting and clinging to Eden, he declared, "This is the best moment of my life."

Finally spent, the three of them remained joined until the men softened and slipped out. Still, they didn't want to let go of one another, so they held on, whispering words of wonder and love to each other. Matty rolled to the side, pulling Eden off of Nico, and the three of them spooned until Eden nearly fell asleep.

"We need to clean up," Nico whispered at last, so he slipped out of bed and returned with a damp towel to take care of his husband and wife. He loved thinking about them that way. The three of them drifted into deep slumber. It had been a long and wonderful day.

A FEW DAYS AFTER THE WEDDING, MATTY DECIDED HE'D better go see Father Andrew to clear the air and make sure there was no misunderstanding. He didn't want Father Andrew to feel horrible, even if he'd been manipulative. Nico and Eden weren't so sure about this idea. They pointed out that although Matty had a heart of gold, not everyone was as giving or forgiving.

Matty heard their concerns, but he firmly believed that the older man had been a valued friend until he'd gone too far. Matty wanted to make sure Father Andrew knew he still cared about the man's feelings.

When Matty arrived at the church, Sister Mary Gertrude was nowhere to be found. The interior door was open, so Matty went straight to Father Andrew's office. He found

Father Andrew there, packing up the contents of his office into wooden crates.

The older man was startled by the sight of Matty standing in his doorway in street clothes. "What are you doing here?" he snarled. "Have you come to gloat?"

"Not at all, Father. I came to see if you were alright."

"I'm not—thanks to you."

"Where are you going?"

"Bishop Morrow has reassigned me to what he has assured me is going to be a 'challenging and exciting new adventure' for me."

"Hmm. That sounds a lot like what you told me when you shipped me off to what felt like jail."

"I was protecting you!"

Matty sighed. "I understand and I'm grateful, but you could have managed that without all of the lying. The classes were good, but the lack of contact with the outside world was stifling. I've made peace with it, though, and I'll be using my education for something wonderful. I wanted you to know that." Matty watched as Father Andrew stuffed some books into a box with a lot more force than was necessary. "So, where are you heading?"

"The diocese is trying to establish more of a Catholic presence in the Mojave Desert of all places, so I'm being sent to build a church in Barstow. Bishop Morrow told me I'd done such a good job working with you during your years of suffering and strife, I was a natural to go work in the desert where I'd no doubt find plenty of worthwhile challenges. He also encouraged me to brush up on my Spanish."

"I wasn't aware you spoke Spanish."

"I don't."

Matty tried to hide his surprise. He knew next to nothing about Barstow—only that it was a new train depot, but the Mojave Desert always sounded to him like hell on earth. He imagined smothering heat and plenty of rattlesnakes. Apparently, the bishop hadn't taken kindly to Father Andrew's subterfuge and cloaked his "assignment" in words that made it sound like a splendid new experience.

"Well then, I wish you the best of luck with your new parish. Who's taking over here?"

"I don't know, but eventually it could have been you if you weren't so pig-headed."

"I never wanted a church, Father. I never wanted to become a priest either. I just went along with the process because I had no other choice and was led to believe some things that weren't true. But now I'm happy to say that I'll be teaching—in a lay capacity—at the Vincentian boys' school where Nico and I were students, and I'm quite pleased about that turn of events. I hope you can be happy for me."

"Delighted. Now if you'll excuse me, I have a lot of packing to do."

Softly, Matty said, "It never would have happened, Father."

The priest looked up sharply at Matty, and the pain in his eyes was clear. "Not if you never gave me… *it*… a chance."

"My heart was always Nico's, and you know it."

"You gave it to him too young. You could have learned… if you had just listened…"

"I'm married to two wonderful people now, Father. I've never been happier. Maybe you can take some joy in that knowledge since you profess to care about me. A truly loving heart is not a selfish one."

Father Andrew grumbled something unintelligible.

"Also, I never wanted to take vows and cast them aside by not remaining celibate. It's just wrong, Father. I cannot lie to God."

Matty realized that Father Andrew had a tear streaking down his cheek, so he reached out and grasped his hand. "Be well, sir. I wish you luck and happiness wherever you go."

Matty turned to leave.

Father Andrew had no reply for him.

Epilogue

True to his promise to Abner Godwin, Nico spoke to his family about the possibility of investing in a cattle ranch. And so it was that Walter became a gentleman rancher. Walter talked them into buying the Hatchett property and leasing it to Eden's family for a small share of profits from the sale of steers at auction. Walter found the whole idea most amusing, even though he didn't expect to make much money from it. He did a lot of reading on the subject of being a cowboy, though, and entertained himself immensely.

Walter also had the Hatchett house razed and built a new one in its place. It gave them somewhere comfortable to stay when they visited the Godwins. During calving season, Nico would always take off a week, then Matty a different week, and anyone else in their household who wanted would accompany them and help out at the ranch as much as possible.

Walter thought it was peaceful riding around on the ranch, looking for stray steers who'd separated from the herd and areas where their fences needed repairs, whereas Nico and Matty participated in more of the backbreaking labor. Once in a while, Isaac would arrive and make repairs for the Godwins when they needed carpentry work done. Warren never showed much interest, but Bay thought it was an enjoyable getaway, and Jeb Hawkins also found out about the family's involvement and showed up now and then. All of these extra hands helped Abner Godwin and his ranch immensely, especially since no one would accept a penny for their labors.

With so many different people coming and going from the Los Angeles branch of the family, no one questioned Matty's relationship to anyone. He was just a friendly, helpful man who showed up and worked hard. The Godwins were too busy to pay much attention anyway.

Eden was happy she'd be able to see her family regularly, especially after little Cora was born. She was named for Matty's late mother. Blonde and bubbly, with enormous blue eyes, she looked like a tiny, girly version of Nico, and she was doted on by the entire household.

In rapid succession after Cora's birth, Eden produced Remy, Louis, Albert, Clifford, and Abraham until Cora complained bitterly to her mother that she wanted a *sister*, and her mother better not have any more boys! A couple of years after Abie's birth, Cora's wish was granted, and baby Shoshanna was born—a tiny replica of her mother. She was the final child for them. All of the children were blue-eyed, and the family speculated now and then about the actual parentage of each of them except for Cora, but no one particularly cared. The children all loved music, but that could have been due to constant exposure rather than genetics.

Matty loved teaching just as much as he'd expected to and became a beloved mentor to many of his students. He started a tradition of having a Roman banquet each year for the Latin students, and that became a lasting school tradition that grew in complexity—and hilarity—each year it was held. All of the attendees wore togas and spoke Latin as much as possible, and when they couldn't find the right Latin translation for their thoughts, they spoke pig Latin. It was always a good laugh that the students looked forward to.

Eden was too busy popping out babies and caring for them to embrace becoming a nurse, though she volunteered some of her time at the clinic handling paperwork. She told her husbands, "I'll do plenty of nursing at home." Indeed, there was always a baby at her breast or a scraped knee to tend to. Her friends who worked for the clinic, however, were greatly appreciated for their hard work and dedication.

Doc Louis retired soon after the arrival of Otto Schubert. Nico and Otto revamped the practice to modernize it and then added two more doctors to their staff. The clinic was a terrific success and greatly needed in such a rapidly growing city.

The Stark-James estate remained a bustling hive of activity, and the house was always filled with music, laughter, and love.

Eden, Nico, and Matty's tripod remained strong and sturdy, supporting each other with grace and devotion.

The End

Have you read the two other books in the Hearts of Gold series?
Book One is The Golden Rush
Jasper, Royal, and Adeline's story

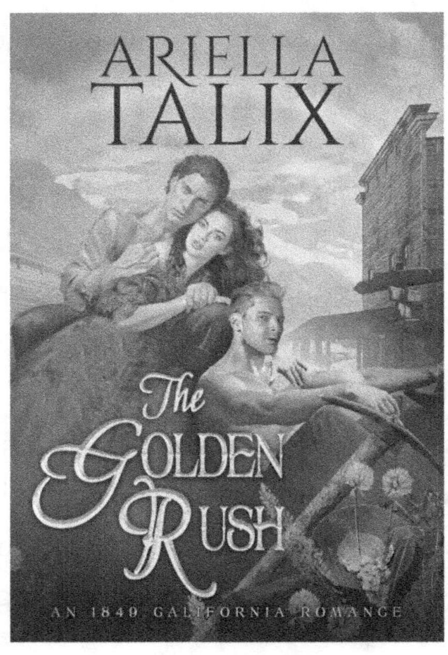

. . .

Book Two is Fiddle and Fire:
Isaac, Walter, and Suzette's story

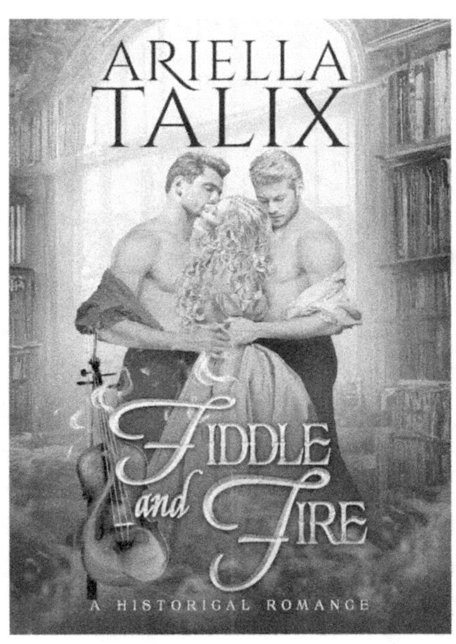

Acknowledgments and Other Thoughts

It was fascinating to see how many inventions eased people's lives between the years of Nico's birth and the beginning of this book when he is sixteen. Electricity was still in its infancy and didn't work all that well, so it was usually combined with gas, though some houses were wired for electricity alone. Indoor plumbing was available to the rich, but since Walter had wanted that since they built The Discovery in *The Golden Rush*, I knew he'd figure out a way to equip their new Los Angeles home. Less obvious items like towels had become popular after being introduced at an 1851 expo. We have a technological boom today that feels like magic sometimes, but imagine how lives changed when, for the first time ever, one could turn on the tap or a light with the flick of a wrist.

The telephone had been invented, of course, but still

required assistance from a switchboard operator, who generally only worked during the day. Operators were scarce, but they did exist, and their use became more and more widespread during the span of this book. If you've read the earlier books in this series, you will remember Walter's obsession with technology and progress. He always wanted the latest and greatest invention. I knew Walter would see to it that they had one as soon as he could, so I was happy to oblige him.

Researching educational opportunities at that time proved challenging because of what the internet seems to think we ought to know rather than what we want to know. Often what I discovered was irrelevant or contradictory, and just because of dumb luck (?) I picked a time period during which things were changing rapidly. A lot of what I needed to have happened came about a few years later. I originally wanted to locate my story where my own family set down roots near San Juan Capistrano. Unfortunately, it was far too rural there for my characters to have thrived, and the local mission was a dilapidated mess until Fr. O'Sullivan (a family friend) took over and had it repaired to its previous glory. It seemed a far better choice for Eden's family ranch, so they settled more or less where my family had a ranch.

As it was for the previous two books in the series, language was always a challenge for me, and a fascinating one. I hope I didn't miss any anachronistic mistakes. Believe me, I tried to avoid them. The origins and timelines of some words were quite eye-opening.

As always, I have to thank my wonderful team of helpers. Dar Albert of Wicked Smart Designs did a wonderful job on this beautiful cover, and cheerfully put up with all of my opinions as we finalized the project. So a million thanks to Dar for that.

My beta reader Susan has been especially helpful on this book. I love that she isn't afraid to say, "Nope!" to some of my ideas and drag me into expanding others that were too abrupt or quick. It's easy to miss the forest for the trees when you're writing, and a careful beta reader like Susan is a special treasure.

Continued thanks to my lovely editor Amy Maranville of Kraken Communications. She always manages to smooth out the rough spots in a terrific way. The result still sounds like me, only better.

I had to get an okay from my proofreader Mattie Davenport of Davenport Edits who has been with me since the beginning of my writing career, and whose opinions I value tremendously. When I named one of the main characters Matty, I didn't even realize I was using her name for a few weeks. Being rather visually driven, the Y instead of the IE didn't register as the same, I guess. I was originally going to call him Mateo, but I kept confusing Nico and Mateo, so he became Matty. And then it turned out that "Matty" was also a close—but sadly departed—friend of my beta reader's. So Matty's name honors two fine people in a good way. I assured Mattie that he was lovable, and not some creepy villain!

Thank you to Mattie for her hard work and for allowing me to use her name.

As always, my husband served as a terrific sounding board for ideas in this book, and I couldn't have done it without him. I also appreciate his patience when writing takes over my brain (and basically all conscious thought), and fixing dinner sometimes is a tiny afterthought. Housework too… but it's hard to get too worked up about that one. Proof in point here… I just had to run downstairs and stick dinner in the oven. I'd have forgotten if I hadn't just written this paragraph. (Edited to add later: I actually put the roast in the oven but neglected to turn it on). Sigh.

Thank you also to Annie Rose and Colleen Noyes for the promotional work I could never manage on my own. They're terrific at what they do.

Thank you to my oddball ancestors who inspired me to write this series. None of the characters represent actual people in my family, but the backbone of the story is there. It began with the Gold Rush and ended in Southern California on a ranch in San Juan Capistrano, as I've mentioned before. I was glad they emigrated south because I didn't want to leave my beloved characters in San Francisco with the approach of the devastating earthquake and fire that decimated the city.

The biggest thanks of all goes to you, dear reader. Without your support and feedback, this would all be for nothing. Thank you for reading my stories and for letting me know your feelings about them. Thank you for telling your friends to read my books and for encouraging me to keep writing them.

I've had plenty of different jobs throughout my life, but I have never loved any career as much as I love being an author.

Books by Ariella Talix

Every book is a standalone story with no cliffhanger.

Each series is more fun when read in order, however. Often characters show up again.

Historical MMF Romance

Hearts of Gold:

The Golden Rush

Fiddle and Fire

Casting Vows

Contemporary Romance

The Drummonds:

Porter the Importer

Make Believe

The Artist

Lovers in Louisville (Spin-off from The Drummonds):

Save Her

Saving Him

Savor This

Contemporary MMF Romance

The Perfect Number (Spin-off from Savor This):

The Rule of 3

The Passion of 3

Living the Fantasy:

Just Curious

Compelling Urges

Standalone:

Group Hug

<u>Charity Anthology</u>

Double Down on Love (Jack of Hearts) with the Kentuckiana
Romance Writers